THE HEIR'S UNEXPECTED RETURN

THE HEIR'S UNEXPECTED RETURN

BY

JACKIE BRAUN

First published in Great Britain 2015
by Mills & Boon, an imprint of Harlequin (UK) Limited,
Large Print edition 2015
Eton House, 18-24 Paradise Road,
Richmond, Surrey, TW9 1SR

ISBN: 978-0-263-25635-2

Harlequin (UK) Limited's policy is to use papers that are natural, renewable and recyclable products and made from wood grown in sustainable forests. The logging and manufacturing processes conform to the legal environmental regulations of the country of origin.

Printed and bound in Great Britain
by CPI Antony Rowe, Chippenham, Wiltshire

For Mark, my real-life hero.

CHAPTER ONE

FAT THUNDERCLOUDS ROLLED overhead and spat rain like machine gun fire as wave after wave battered Hadley Island's sandy beachfront. As it was on one of the barrier islands off the South Carolina coast, the sixteen-mile-long stretch of pristine shoreline was used to the abuse. Mother Nature's fury, however, was no match for the emotions roiling inside Brigit Wright.

Unmindful of the worsening storm, she continued to walk. In the pocket of the yellow rain slicker she wore, she fisted her hand around the already-crumpled piece of paper. Printing out the email hadn't changed its content.

Miss Wright, I will be arriving home the day after tomorrow for an extended stay. Please have my quarters on the main floor ready.
—KF

Two curt sentences that still had her blood boiling.

Kellen Faust, heir to the Faust fortune, was returning coming "home" as he'd put it—to continue his recuperation after the skiing accident he'd suffered four months earlier in the Swiss Alps.

If the news reports she'd read about his fall were even remotely accurate, then Brigit supposed she should feel sorry for him. Along with a concussion, dislocated shoulder and broken wrist, he'd snapped his ankle, mangled his knee and shattered the femur in his right leg. Four months out and the man was still in the midst of a long and very painful recovery. Even so, she didn't want him here while he did his mending, potentially meddling in the day-to-day minutia of running the exclusive Faust Haven resort. Brigit preferred to work without interference.

Kellen's family had a large home outside Charleston, as well as an assortment of plush real estate holdings sprinkled around Europe. Why hadn't he picked one of those places to do his recuperating? Surely they would be more accommodating to Kellen's large entourage and the other assorted sycophants who enabled his Peter Pan–like existence.

Why choose Faust Haven? This wasn't his home. It was *hers*, dammit! Just as Faust Haven was *her* resort, the name on the deed notwithstanding. While he'd spent the past five years hotfooting around Europe, living off what had to be a sizable trust fund and enjoying the life of the idle rich, Brigit had been hard at work turning a tired and nearly forgotten old-money retreat into a fashionable, five-star accommodation that offered excellent service and amenities and, above all else, discretion, in addition to its panoramic views. As such it was booked solid not only for the current calendar year, but for the next three. Brigit had made that happen. And she'd done so without Kellen's help.

Now the heir was returning and he wanted his quarters readied. *His* quarters? During the time she'd managed the resort, Kellen had never set foot on the island. It was Brigit's understanding that he hadn't visited the island since he was a boy. So she'd made the owner's private apartment on the main floor her own, and had turned the manager's rooms into a luxury suite that commanded a handsome sum.

Where was she going to sleep now? She might go to bed after most of the guests were tucked in for the night and rise long before they awoke, but that didn't mean she wanted to bunk on one of the overstuffed couches in the lobby or the big leather recliner in the library, no matter how comfy she found it to be for reading.

Muttering an oath that was swallowed by the wind, she stopped walking and looked back in the direction she had come. The cedar-shingled resort stood three stories tall—four, really, given the pilings that raised it another twelve feet above sea level to protect it from flooding. Natural sand dunes dotted with clumps of gangly grass buffered the structure from the worst of the Atlantic's abuse.

Home.

Kellen might refer to it as such, but for Brigit that truly was the case. It was here she'd come after her nasty divorce. Pride battered, feeling like an epic failure. The sea air, the sense of purpose, both had played a key role in ushering her back from the brink of despair.

Her gaze skimmed the balconies that stretched out from every room to maximize the view. Even though it was early afternoon, the lights burned brightly in the windows, beacons of welcome to any guests who had braved the worsening weather and boarded the last ferry from the mainland before the storm halted service. Once travelers reached the island, of course, they would still have to navigate the winding roads over the hilly center of Hadley Island to the eastern shore where the resort was situated. But even accounting for the slow going, those guests would be arriving soon.

With a sigh, Brigit headed back. She had a job to do and she would do it. Right now, her priority was to see that all new arrivals were comfortably settled in their rooms. Once that task was accomplished, she would work on figuring out her own accommodations for the duration of Kellen's stay.

By the time she reached the resort, any part of her body not covered by the slicker was drenched.

She had hoped to have enough time to change into dry clothes and do something with her hair before the first guests arrived, but a full-size black SUV was pulling up under the covered portico at the main entrance as she came around the dune.

The driver hopped out, as did another man, who came around from the vehicle's passenger side. Both were big and burly. Bodyguards? It wasn't a surprise. A lot of the inn's guests were important people—Hollywood A-listers, business magnates, politicians. Before either man could reach for the handle, however, the rear passenger door swung open.

Brigit covered her mouth, but a gasp still escaped.

Kellen Faust. The heir was early.

She'd never met Kellen in person. They exchanged emails and texts a couple times a month, and occasionally a phone call. But he'd never come for a visit. Now here he was. In the flesh. And he wasn't at all what Brigit had expected.

Every photograph she had seen of him—and the guy turned up in print and online media reports with as much regularity as the tide—showed a handsome young man with sun-lightened brown hair, deep-set hazel eyes, a carefree smile and a body honed to perfection under what had to be the capable tutelage of a well-paid personal trainer.

Meanwhile, the man trying to exit the SUV's rear seat was thin, borderline gaunt, muscles withered away from long hours spent still and sedated. The dark smudges under his eyes made it plain he hadn't been getting much sleep as of late. He remained good-looking, but if his rigid posture and pinched features were any indication, he was far from carefree.

Vital, healthy, fit? None of the descriptions she'd seen in press clippings applied to the man now.

"I'll get the wheelchair, Mr. Faust," said the man who'd come around from the front passenger side.

"No! I'll walk," he bit out in an angry rasp that carried to Brigit despite the howling wind.

"But, Mr. Faust—" the driver began, only to be shouted down.

"I said I'll walk, Lou! I'm *not* a freaking invalid!"

Kellen swung his left leg out the door without too much effort, but when it came to the right one, he had to use his hands to manipulate the limb over the threshold. Then, lowering himself to the running board first, he eased to the ground. He held a cane in one hand. He used the other hand to grip the door frame. Unfortunately, neither support was enough to save him. A mere second after both of his feet hit the driveway, his right knee buckled. The man he'd called Lou caught Kellen under his arms before he hit the pavement. Ripe cursing followed. The other man rushed forward, as did Brigit, determined to help.

"Who in the hell are you?" Kellen bellowed, shaking off the hand she placed on his arm.

She pushed back her hood and offered what she hoped was a professional smile. Wouldn't it just figure that she looked her absolute worst for the occasion? Despite the rain slicker's hood, her hair was damp, and the bangs that she was three months into growing out were plastered against her forehead. As for makeup, she doubted the little bit she'd applied that morning lingered on her eyelashes and cheeks now. Her feet were bare, her calves spattered with wet sand. It was hardly the professional image she'd planned to portray when she first made his acquaintance.

"I'm Brigit Wright." When he continued to stare as if she were something to be studied on a slide under a microscope, she added, "We've spoken on the phone and via email for, well, several years. I manage Faust Haven."

That news elicited not a polite smile, but a snort that bordered on derisive.

"Of course you do." His gaze flickered down in seeming dismissal. Although he said it half under his breath, she heard him well enough when he added, "I had you pegged right."

So, the man had preconceived notions of her, did he? That didn't come as much of a surprise. And to be fair, she entertained plenty of her own where he was concerned. Still, it irked her that, after a mere glance, he could so easily marginalize her—both professionally and, she didn't doubt, personally.

Brigit cleared her throat and drew herself up to her full height of five foot six. Since he was hunched over, it put them nearly at eye level. When their gazes connected she didn't so much as blink. Using her most practiced "boss" tone, she told him, "I wasn't expecting you. Your email, which I received only this morning, said you wouldn't arrive until the day after tomorrow."

"I changed my mind."

"Obviously."

"I was in Charleston visiting..." His words trailed off and his expression hardened. "I'm here now. I trust that's not a problem, Miss Wright."

"None whatsoever," she assured him with a stiff smile. "I just wanted to explain that your *quarters,* well, they are not ready at the moment."

"Am I expected to wait out here until they are?" he demanded irritably.

Standing under the portico, they were protected from the worst of the rain, but the wind pushed enough of it sideways that it splattered them every now and again.

"Of course not," she replied as heat crept into

her cheeks. What was she thinking, keeping a guest of his position, much less his current condition, out in the elements? She turned on her heel and marched toward the lobby entrance, calling over her shoulder, "Right this way, gentlemen."

Kellen didn't follow the ever-efficient Miss Wright inside to the elevator. Rather, he allowed Lou and Joe to half drag, half carry him in the direction of the door. He'd ticked her off but good. No surprise that, since he'd been so rude. Another time, he would have felt bad about the way he'd treated her. Unfortunately for her, both his usual good humor and his abundant charm had gone the way of his right leg. That was to say, fractured beyond repair. Or so the doctors claimed. They were wrong. They had to be. He couldn't spend the rest of his life like this…barely able to walk. A mere shadow of the healthy, active man he used to be.

The elevator doors opened after a bell dinged, announcing their arrival. The lobby looked different than he remembered from the last time he'd been to Faust Haven. Gone were the deep green, gold and maroon that had always struck him as more suited to a Rocky Mountains cabin than an ocean-side resort. Varying shades of blue and turquoise dominated the color scheme now, accentuated with weathered white and a pale yellow that reminded Kellen of sand. Overhead lights, along with the glow of table lamps, gave the lobby a warm, welcoming ambiance despite the storm that raged outside.

He exhaled slowly, and some of the tension left his shoulders. He remained a long way from relaxed, but he knew one thing for certain. He'd been right to come here.

He'd been second-guessing the decision to leave Switzerland ever since his plane touched down in Raleigh and the only one to greet him at the airport had been his mother's ancient butler holding a hand-lettered sign bearing Kellen's name. Orley hadn't changed much, but Kellen apparently had. The older man hadn't recognized him. Of course, it had been nearly a dozen years since Kellen had set foot in his boyhood home in Charleston.

And it had been longer than that since he'd been to the island.

He glanced around again. "This is…this is nice," he said to no one in particular.

"The remodeling was completed last fall. All of the guest rooms have been updated in a similar color scheme." She cleared her throat. Her tone was just this side of defensive when she added, "I emailed you numerous photographs."

He didn't remember the photos. He probably hadn't bothered to open the attachments. Too busy burning through his trust fund to care, he thought with a mental grimace. Well, he was done with that. In a way, the accident had forced his hand. He couldn't ignore his responsibilities any longer. It was time to put his degree to use and start earning his keep.

"They didn't do it justice," he murmured.

Nor, Kellen admitted, had the image he'd had in his head done her justice, despite what he'd just said about having her pegged.

For the past five years, he'd signed her paychecks, given the reports she'd dutifully sent on the first of each month a quick skim and approved her capital improvements—all while offering minimal input. This had been accomplished remotely. He'd never laid eyes on the woman to whom he'd entrusted what was now all that was left of to his birthright…until now.

She'd shed the old-man-and-the-sea rain slicker and stood in front of the reception desk wearing an aqua-blue polo shirt adorned with the inn's logo and a pair of white shorts that skimmed to mid-thigh. Nice legs—tanned, toned and surprisingly long for someone who probably topped out at five and a half feet. His gaze lifted to her waist, which was small, before rising to her breasts, which were just the right size to fill a man's hands.

He tore his gaze away, surprised to find himself ogling the woman—his employee no less—as if he were some sort of sex-crazed frat boy on spring break. At the same time, he was a bit relieved by his reaction, as base as it was. He'd felt dead for so long…

"I need to get off my feet, Miss Wright. Sooner rather than later, if you don't mind." Pain turned his tone surly.

“Of course.” She gave a curt nod. “Follow me.”

Pride demanded that he do so under his own steam, as slow as that would make the going. He took his cane from his driver before turning to Joe.

“Help Lou with the bags.”

Officially, Joe was his physical therapist, but the younger man didn’t mind pitching in as an extra pair of hands when needed. He was being paid well enough, and it wasn’t as if he was kept particularly busy since Kellen regularly skipped his daily stretching and strengthening workouts.

He knew he needed to do them, of course. But knowing and doing were two different things. Hell, some days, Kellen was lucky to get out of bed at all, especially when specialist after specialist offered such a grim prognosis.

He shifted from his good leg to the bad one. Even using the cane to bear much of his weight, the pain was excruciating. He bit back a groan and wondered for the millionth time if it had been wise to swear off the narcotics his doctor prescribed, even if they had made him dizzy and brain-dead. Even if secretly he’d worried that the lure of oblivion might prove too much and he would wind up addicted.

His progress was slow, his gait uneven and lurching, although at least he was able to bear his weight. Brigit turned around once, concern obvious in her expression, but she didn't offer any assistance. Even when he stumbled before catching his balance, she kept her distance and said nothing. Apparently, his rude dismissal of her help outside had done the trick. He was glad for that. Kellen hated the way people were always rushing to his aid, opening doors, clearing a path for him. For the invalid. Hell, he was surprised they didn't try to wipe his mouth or other parts of his anatomy as if he were a damn baby.

Women had been among the worst offenders. That was one of the reasons he'd ditched the entourage of females that had routinely crashed at his chalet. As for his male friends, the number had dwindled to nil once it had become clear Kellen no longer would be throwing any of the parties for which he had become legend.

Users and hangers-on, every last one of them. What did it say about him, Kellen wondered, that the only loyalty he commanded was among people such as Joe and Lou and, yeah, Miss Wright, all of whom were on his payroll?

Behind the reception desk, a door led to a short hallway. To the left were the business office, supply room and laundry facility. Kellen remembered playing hide-and-seek in them as a boy during visits with his grandfather. The employee break room was new. He didn't ask about it, though. No doubt she'd told him about its addition in one of those emails he'd barely skimmed.

The owner's two-bedroom apartment was on the right. The door was closed, the word *private* stamped on a plaque affixed just below a peephole. After Brigit pulled a key from her pocket and opened it, Kellen stepped over the threshold, prepared to be assailed with memories of his grandfather, the one person in his life whose love had been complete and unconditional. But as in the lobby, nothing here was as he remembered. Given how emotional he already was feeling, he wasn't sure whether he was grateful for that or not.

The last time Kellen had been inside, the decor

had been far more masculine. It wasn't only the pale, almost pastel shades of paint on the walls that made it seem feminine now. It was the furnishings: overstuffed white couch, patterned throw pillows, decorative lamps, fat candles in ornate holders, glass jars filled with an assortment of seashells that he'd bet Brigit had collected herself. The scent that lingered in the air was not that of his grandfather's pipe tobacco. Rather, it was light, fresh and pretty. Her scent. He inhaled deeply, finding it oddly comforting and arousing at the same time. He shoved the unsettling thought aside, only to have another take its place.

"You live here."

She frowned. "For the past few years, yes. Room and board are one of the perks of the job."

"I know that. But this was my grandfather's apartment. It's for the owner… I didn't realize."

"You didn't realize?" Her tone was as incredulous as her expression. "But I told you—"

He cut her off. "I thought there was an apartment on the other side of the lobby to accommodate the manager."

Brigit's mouth puckered at his response, drawing Kellen's attention to a pair of lush lips that needed no added color to make them appealing, despite the agitation reflected in her eyes.

"There is, or rather, there was. But since this apartment was just sitting empty all the time, I… that is, *we* decided it made more sense to turn the manager's apartment into a luxury suite that could accommodate four or more guests for an extended stay."

"*We* did?"

Color rose in her cheeks. He was surprised he couldn't see steam waft from her crown. "I sent you several reports listing the pros and cons. You said you agreed with the cost-benefit analysis that I supplied when I first made the suggestion."

"Right. I remember now." Kellen nodded, although he was damned if he could recall doing any such thing.

She'd taken excellent care of the inn. Every penny invested in capital improvements had paid off, he decided, thinking of the lobby. Whereas he had been reckless in the past, the risks Brigit took had been calculated and well thought out.

He might have approved her plans, but the decisions had been hers alone. Kellen had a business degree. One that he'd never earned a living from…although he planned to do so now. He'd be wise to pay attention, learn the ropes from what was obviously a very competent manager.

"It's been full ever since," she added.

Which meant it was full now.

Kellen appreciated her ability to turn previously unused space profitable, but it did make for a tricky situation. "Where are you going to sleep, Miss Wright?"

Where was she going to sleep?

Brigit gritted her teeth. That was the million-dollar question, but she shrugged and offered what she hoped passed for an unconcerned smile.

"I'll figure out something for the duration of your stay." As unspecified as that might be. And as short as she hoped it would turn out.

Kellen lumbered to the couch and dropped heavily onto the cushions, his face pinched with a grimace. Sheer will had kept him upright, of that much she was certain. She might have admired his tenacity if it weren't accompanied by such a surly disposition.

"Well, there must be at least one guest room available, right?" For the first time, he sounded more uncertain than he did irascible.

"No. Full means full. And we're full this week."

"And next?"

She exhaled slowly. "Actually, for the rest of the season barring any last-minute cancellations." When he just continued to gape at her, she added, "It's been an excellent summer so far. Revenues are up by—"

He cut her off with a ripe oath. "Well, you can't sleep in the damned lobby."

Brigit already had made the same determination, but her options were limited. The only alternative was…

Her gaze cut to the hallway and the spare bedroom, where she exercised when the weather prevented her from getting outside for a run. It had a futon that pulled out into what her older sister claimed was a pretty comfortable bed. Robbie and her son, Will, were the only overnight guests Brigit had ever entertained. On a sigh, she recalled their upcoming visit. She'd have to let them know plans had changed. Yet another disruption in her otherwise well-organized schedule.

"I'll have our bellboy set up a cot for me in the office," she said at last.

"The office we just passed?" He snorted. "It's barely big enough for the desk. You can't get a bed in there, even if it is a damn cot."

"It will be tight," she admitted. Not to mention that she would need to figure out where to shower and stow her belongings, but at least it would afford her more privacy than the inn's common areas.

"No."

She blinked. "No?"

"No." This time his tone made the single syllable sound even more final.

Brigit felt her blood pressure rise again. The man certainly knew how to push her buttons. She didn't like being told what to do. Since her divorce, no man had dared, nor would she have stood for it. After her fiasco of a marriage, during which she had all but disappeared behind her husband's overbearing and autocratic personality, she'd vowed never to become invisible or obsolete again. She had a brain and a voice. These days, she used both with impunity.

But just as she opened her mouth to protest, Kellen leaned his head back on the sofa and closed his eyes. Dressed in varying shades of gray and black—colors that mirrored his mood—she couldn't help but notice how out of place he looked amid the array of cheerful throw pillows. Still, she might have argued with his edict. Firmly but politely, of course, since he was her employer and tact was in order. But his expression stopped her. The taut line of his mouth and the way his brow furrowed made it plain that he was hurting.

"When was the last time you took a painkiller?" she asked. She kept her tone neutral, careful to keep any concern from leaking into it lest she knick his pride. From the way he'd shrugged off her assistance earlier, she gathered he didn't want any.

Men. It was all she could do not to roll her

eyes. She'd thought she was done stroking their damned egos now that Scott was out of the picture. Well, apparently not.

"I quit those a few weeks ago," he muttered. Just when she started to think his decision was rooted in some sort of macho tough-guy bull, he added, "They make me a zombie. It's not all that unpleasant of a feeling, but the last thing I need is to wind up addicted to pain meds on top of everything else."

His reasoning was sound, even if it meant his pain was left unmanaged.

The two men who'd accompanied Kellen strode into the apartment then. The driver was hauling a pair of suitcases that were large enough to hold Brigit's entire wardrobe. The younger man pushed the wheelchair. A smaller piece of luggage was balanced on its seat with a garment bag draped over top of it. Brigit's stomach dropped. Kellen had brought a lot of baggage—in more ways than one. And none of it boded well for how long she would be displaced from her home.

"Where do you want your things, boss?" the driver asked.

Without opening his eyes, Kellen motioned with one hand in the direction of the hall. "Put them in the master bedroom, Lou."

"And mine?" the guy pushing the wheelchair asked.

Kellen did open his eyes now and he straightened in his seat. "Change of plans, Joe. Miss Wright will be bunking in the spare room. You'll be out here on the couch."

Brigit's mouth fell open. Just like that, he'd turned them all into roommates.

CHAPTER TWO

AGAIN, BRIGIT TRIED to protest. “That’s not necessary. As I said, I can sleep on a cot in the office.”

“And I say it is necessary.” Kellen waved a hand. Then, “Not to be rude, but if you could move your belongings out of your room into the spare and be on your way, I’d appreciate it. I need to lie down.”

He didn’t wait for Brigit to respond. Rather, he returned his head to the cushion and closed his eyes once again.

She’d been dismissed like the hired help she was. Well, hired help or not, his dismissal made her blood boil. It took an effort, but she managed to swallow the pithy reply that likely would have seen her fired. Instead, as she followed the pair of burly men down the hall, she muttered half under her breath, “Sure, Mr. Faust. No problem, Mr. Faust. Happy to oblige.”

Brigit kept a tidy home, even in the rooms that casual visitors normally didn't see. She was grateful for that fact now that strangers were invading her privacy.

Although the rooms were neat, she would have to change the sheets on her bed before Kellen used it. She'd planned to handle that chore in the morning, as well as gather up her clothes and toiletries in anticipation of his arrival. By showing up a day and a half early, and bringing another overnight guest, he'd left her scrambling and feeling…inadequate.

She swallowed the bile that threatened to inch up the back of her throat. The sentiment didn't sit well.

While the driver continued down the hall, Brigit stopped at the first doorway. Glancing around the spare room, she tapped a finger to her lips. The treadmill would need to be moved to the corner to make room to open the futon, which would need fresh linens. Ditto for the living room's pullout couch, where Kellen had assigned Joe to bunk.

As if reading her mind, Joe said from behind

her, "Sorry for all of the inconvenience our stay is causing you."

She turned, taking in his sheepish smile. She guessed him to be a few years her junior, which would put him in his late twenties. Despite a hairline that was already receding halfway across his crown, his face was almost boyish. If he had to shave once a week, she would be surprised.

"It's no problem," she lied.

"I'm Joe Bosley, your other uninvited guest." He let go of one of the wheelchair handles so he could shake her hand. "I'm Mr. Faust's physical therapist."

"It's nice to meet you, Joe. I'm Brigit Wright. As you probably guessed, I manage Faust Haven."

Joe nodded. Then, "Hey, would it be okay if I stowed my stuff in here?"

Better in the spare room with her than taking up space in the main living area. Brigit nodded and then pointed across the room. "The drawers in that dresser are mostly empty. If you'd like, you can have a couple of them."

"Great. Thanks. I'll take the bottom two."

That left her with the top three. "And there's plenty of room in the closet if you have anything you want to hang up."

"Nah." Joe wrinkled his pug-like nose and motioned to his hulking frame. "I'm a wash-and-wear kind of guy. Shorts, T-shirts and sweats mostly, although I do keep a pair of khaki pants and a few polo shirts on hand for anything that requires me to dress up."

She nearly smiled. Khakis and collared shirts were Joe's formal wear. Meanwhile, if all of the photographs she'd seen of Kellen over the years were any indication, the guy probably owned stock in Armani. *Not that Kellen didn't wear a tux well*, a traitorous voice whispered. She silenced it.

Joe's simple wardrobe explained why he had only one medium-size suitcase while his boss had brought a pair of ginormous ones as well as a garment bag. Whatever designer-label duds were stuffed inside of them really wasn't the issue. The sheer amount said he was planning a far more extended stay than she'd first assumed. Just her luck.

"This is a nightmare," she muttered, momentarily forgetting about her audience.

Not surprisingly, Joe misunderstood what she meant. "You'll hardly know we're here."

"I'm sorry. That was rude. I'm not usually rude," she said.

Uptight, unimaginative and colossally boring both in the bedroom and out, according to her ex, but even that jerk had never called Brigit's manners into question.

"It's okay." Joe sent her a reassuring smile. Then, motioning over his shoulder with one thumb, he added, "He's not so bad, you know."

"I'm sure." Her attempt at sounding convincing fell far short.

"Really," Joe insisted. "Mr. F is in a lot of pain right now."

She nodded. "He said he's not taking the meds the doctor prescribed. Said they give him brain fog."

She decided to keep to herself the part about him worrying about becoming addicted.

"They'd give an elephant brain fog." Joe leaned closer then and dropped his voice to barely above a whisper. "His pain isn't all physical, although I doubt he'd admit to that."

So, the accident had taken an emotional toll as well. Brigit supposed she shouldn't find that surprising. Even strong people could succumb to depression. God knew, she'd hovered at its dark door for a time just before finally calling it quits on her marriage.

"Mr. Faust's injury…how bad is it?"

"To be honest, it's one of the worst I've ever seen. His wrist and shoulder have healed pretty well, but his leg…he mangled it but good. Major tendon and ligament damage in addition to the bone fractures." Joe shook his head and exhaled. "You know, the doctors initially advised amputating just above the knee."

"My God!" Brigit gasped. "I had no idea."

"Yeah, well, he managed to keep that much from being leaked to the press. His *friends*…" Joe snorted, as if finding the word laughable. "They forwarded all sorts of information and even a few photographs snapped in Mr. F's hospital room to the tabloids. He wasn't happy about it."

"I'd say he needs a better class of friends."

Joe grunted at her assessment. "I can't say I was sorry when he announced we would be heading back to the States. Some of them probably haven't noticed he's gone, although they'll get the idea once the chalet sells."

Brigit's stomach dropped. "Sells?"

"He said he doesn't want to go back there. Of course, it might just be the depression talking."

One could hope. Because if he didn't go back there, she had the sickening feeling she knew where he might next call home.

"How's his therapy going?" she asked, hoping for good news.

That wasn't what she got.

"Slow." Joe sighed. "All of the scar tissue isn't helping, especially since most days he doesn't want to do his exercises."

"That must make your job difficult."

"It does. It also feeds his frustration, because depressed or not, he refuses to give up hope."

"Of walking without assistance, you mean?" she inquired.

Joe nodded. "Walking without assistance to

start. Then running, skiing. He wants to be as good as new."

Despite a mangled leg that the doctors had wanted to amputate.

"That's not likely to happen, is it?" she asked softly.

Joe looked away and cleared his throat. "I really shouldn't be talking about Mr. F's case with anyone. I just wanted you to know that, well, he's not being a jerk right now just to be a jerk."

"Understood. Thank you."

But if Joe thought she was going to cut the irritable Kellen Faust some slack, he was wrong. Oh, she would tread lightly. She wasn't an idiot, and she loved this job. But letting people get away with being insufferable, even if they had a good reason for being that way, wasn't healthy for anyone. Besides, she was finished being anyone's verbal punching bag.

When Brigit reached the master bedroom, the driver was waiting for her. Kellen's large suitcases were open on the bed.

"I'll need a few drawers in the bureau where I can put away his things. Hope that's okay?"

Where Kellen ordered, his employees asked. She appreciated their restraint.

"Sure." She grabbed a tote bag from the closet and started to fill it with socks and underwear from the top drawer. Over her shoulder she called, "I'll be out of your hair in a minute."

The man sported a shaved head, so her phrasing earned a wry look.

"No rush, Miss Wright."

"Call me Brigit."

He smiled, showing off a gold front tooth. "I'm Lou."

"So, Lou, where will you be staying? I assume you won't be bunking in here. Will you and Joe be flipping a coin to see who sleeps on the floor and who gets the pullout sofa?"

"Nah." Lou chuckled. "The kid gets the living room all to himself. I have family on the other side of the island not far from the ferry docks. I'll be staying there, although I'll be on call for the duration of Mr. Faust's stay." He grinned and sent her a wink. "Worried that you were going to have to make room for another unexpected boarder?"

"Not at all. The more the merrier," she said drily.

They both laughed.

While she finished filling her bag with clothes from the dresser drawers, Lou hung an assortment of shirts and pants in the closet. All of the garments screamed expensive and were far more formal than the nylon pants, T-shirt and track jacket Kellen had on now.

Did he plan to wear them? If so, when? Where? Once again, she was left with the uneasy feeling that her employer was hunkering down for the long haul.

The man was accustomed to a robust social life, if the press accounts were to be believed. Well, he wouldn't find much of that on the island. Of course, since his accident, he'd lain low. In recent months, the only time his photograph had graced the newspapers, whether the legitimate press or the gossip rags, he'd been shown leaving a doctor's office or a hospital. No smiles for the cameras in those pictures. He'd worn the same pain-induced grimace she'd viewed firsthand. And his palms had been up, as if to ward off the swarming paparazzi.

Brigit finished clearing out the drawers and hastily grabbed a selection of outfits from the closet, which she took to the spare room. Joe had finished emptying his lone suitcase. Hands on his hips, he was glancing around.

"Can I help you with something?" she asked.

"I've got some equipment I need to bring in for Mr. F's sessions. Some of it is going to take up space. I don't think you're going to want it in the living room."

He was right about that. "The inn has a gym on the main floor. It's small, but there should be room for your equipment."

"Mr. F prefers privacy."

Brigit nodded. She couldn't blame him for that. She preferred privacy herself. Not that she would be getting much of it for the next who-knew-how-long.

"If I have my treadmill moved to storage, will that be enough space? The bookshelf under the window can go, too."

Joe squinted, as if visualizing the room sans

the items she'd mentioned. "Yeah. I think that will do it."

"Great. I'll call the bellboy."

"No need. Lou and I can handle this."

"All right." That settled, she nodded toward the bag that was still on the wheelchair's seat. "Is that Mr. Faust's?"

"Yes."

"I can take that to the master bedroom, if you'd like. I still need to get my toiletries from the bath."

"Appreciate it." Joe handed it to her. Then, "Speaking of toiletries, I take it the two of us will be sharing the bathroom in the hall."

Brigit managed to squelch a groan. The invasion of her privacy was officially complete. Still, if she had to share a bathroom, she supposed she'd rather do so with an affable Joe rather than a sullen Kellen. The latter would be too…intimate.

Where had that thought come from?

She forced a smile and, striving for good humor, asked Joe, "So, are you neat?"

"I can be when the situation calls for it."

"Trust me. It does," she replied drily.

"Then I promise I'll do my best to remember to put the toilet seat down, too."

Brigit's laughter was cut short by a snort coming from the living room. Then Kellen yelled, "Can you two skip the chitchat and finish up? As I'm the one who signs both of your paychecks, I know you have better things to do with your time than flirt."

Flirt! Brigit felt her face flame, but it wasn't merely embarrassment that brought heat rushing into her cheeks. The nerve of the man accusing her of flirting, as if her spending a few minutes talking to a colleague meant she was some sort of slacker. And to think mere minutes earlier she'd started to feel sorry for him based on the extent of his injury. Every ounce of sympathy had evaporated now.

Joe pulled a face. "Sorry," he mouthed.

Brigit nodded, but she was too damned irritated to be sorry.

She delivered the bag to the master bedroom. While Lou and Joe moved the treadmill and bookshelf to storage to make room for the physical therapy equipment, she changed the sheets on the bed where Kellen would sleep. Afterward, she gathered up her toiletries from the attached bathroom and put out fresh hand and bath towels. Then, satisfied that everything was in order, she turned to leave only to do an about-face.

"Toothbrush," she muttered aloud.

She opened the medicine cabinet, planning to grab the item in question. When her gaze landed on the bottle of extra-strength ibuprofen, an idea formed. One that she couldn't resist. She fished the eyeliner pencil out of her makeup bag and, after jotting her message, grinned at her reflection in the mirror.

As Brigit entered the living room, she braced for an unpleasant exchange.

Be polite. Be professional. But hold to your principles.

She needn't have bothered with the internal pep talk. Kellen was fast asleep on her couch. He remained seated where he had been, but his bad leg was propped on the coffee table, one of her colorful pillows under the heel serving as a cushion. In sleep he appeared less formidable and intimidating than he had while glowering at her and barking out orders. But even in slumber he wore a grimace that pulled down the corners of his mouth. Pain. Add in a wheelchair and cane, and it should have made him seem vulnerable. Only none of that did.

Nor did it detract from his overall good looks. With his chiseled cheekbones and square jaw, the man was classically handsome. No getting around that, even in his diminished physical state. Nor was there any getting around his reputation as a freewheeling ladies' man. A lot of women probably thought his polished looks and well-padded bank account made him quite a catch. Especially if they were able to excuse his nasty disposition, she thought uncharitably.

Kellen's head was canted sideways in a position that was sure to leave his neck sore when he awoke. Even so, she didn't attempt to wake him. She had no desire to poke a sleeping bear. Instead, she tiptoed past him, eager to avoid further unpleasantness. At the door, she chanced a glance back. The less interaction Brigit had with her boss, the better.

Kellen woke to the sound of a door closing. He straightened on the couch and craned his neck to one side and then the other. In the short time he'd been asleep, a crick already had formed just below the base of his skull. He grunted. Yet another sore muscle for Joe to work on during their afternoon session. If Kellen went. Maybe he'd skip it again. What was the point, anyway?

It was this kind of thinking that made him angry, even as it also left him feeling defeated. He wanted to get better, but what if he never did? What if all of the medical experts were right?

Kellen rose unsteadily to his feet, bearing as much of his weight as possible on the cane. Damned thing. He hated using it. Hated that he *had* to use it. But most of all, he hated what it represented. It shouted to the world that Kellen Faust was no longer the man he used to be. He was injured, limited.

Useless.

The very thing his own mother had always accused him of being.

The conversation they'd had not long after he'd arrived at her home in Charleston sprang to mind.

"The only thing you're good at is spending money. You've all but drained your trust, living high on the hog in Europe. No cares, no responsibilities." She'd waved one of her bejeweled hands, the diamonds her second husband had given her winking under the lights. "Well, don't expect me to bail you out. You're just like your father. You've never planned for a rainy day."

They were estranged, had been since he was a boy, really. Since not long after his father's lengthy illness and death had left them nearly penniless. She'd come back stronger than ever thanks to remarrying well, but not before hocking almost everything of value to stay afloat. As his grandfather's sole heir, Kellen had been well provided for. In a way, that had only made her resent him, especially since he'd continued his father's free-spending ways. As a result, Kellen and his mother had never shared a close bond again. He'd been foolish to think things might have changed either because of his injury or his changing financial situation.

But he hadn't been wrong to come to Hadley Island. He'd come here to find a purpose, if not a vocation then an avocation. Something, *anything*, to give his life meaning if it turned out that all of the doctors, including the latest one in Charleston, were right.

The best memories of his childhood were rooted here. The place had been his sanctuary, both during his father's illness and after his father's death. Where his relationship with his mother had always been rocky, a young Kellen had been the apple of his grandfather's eye.

"You're bright, ambitious. You're going to be a fine man when you grow up, Kellen."

He wondered what his grandfather would think if he could see Kellen now. The bum leg wouldn't be an issue. But what Kellen had made of his life to this point…that wouldn't sit well with the old man. Granddad had placed his trust in Kellen, left him his fortune and all of his real estate holdings, not the least of which was the resort.

These days, most of what Kellen still owned of his grandfather's had been mortgaged to the hilt and would soon go on the auction block to pay off his mounting, post-accident debts. Except for the inn. Kellen had left that untouched.

"Everything I have will be yours someday." Kellen could hear his granddad's raspy voice, feel the hand he'd placed on his grandson's shoulder as he'd made the promise. "I know you'll take extra good care of the inn, because you love it as much as I do."

Guilt settled over Kellen now like a smothering fog. Yeah, he'd loved it so much that he hadn't been back in nearly a dozen years, and had rubber-stamped renovations without paying close attention to the plans. Thank God Brigit was so good at her job. The managers before her had been more than happy to stick with the status quo, shrugging their shoulders as the bottom line fell. She'd shored up the aging resort and had brought in record profits as well.

When all was said and done, Kellen would see to it that she was properly compensated.

"Do you need anything, Mr. F?" The question

came from Joe, who, with Lou's help, was bringing in a portable table and the weight bench Kellen thought of as a personal torture device.

I'll take a new leg, some motivation and a renewed sense of purpose, he thought bitterly. But what he told the younger man was, "I'm going to lie down for a little while."

Joe frowned at him. "Do you think that's a good idea, Mr. F? Your muscles are probably stiff from the drive over, especially since we didn't get in a session this morning."

Joe was being diplomatic. His wording made it sound as if the omission of the a.m. therapy session had been an oversight rather than because Kellen had refused to cooperate. Hell, he'd refused to get out of bed. Well, at least Joe wasn't mentioning the evening before when Kellen had called it quits a mere five minutes into basic stretches using a tension band.

"I'm going to lie down," Kellen repeated, heading in the direction of the bedroom.

Joe lifted his shoulders as if to say suit yourself.

Lou cleared his throat. "As soon as we finish

unloading this gear, I'm going to take off. That okay with you?"

Lou had been with Kellen for more than a decade, mainly working as his driver—more often designated than not. Sometimes he also stepped into the role of bouncer when party guests got out of control. There hadn't been much need for the latter services the past four months. Kellen's partying days were over. Truth be told, they'd lasted longer than they should have even before the accident.

"This mishap of yours might be for the best," his mother had said just that morning.

"Mishap?" He'd motioned with his cane. "I didn't fall down a couple stairs."

No, more like he'd tumbled head over skis down the side of an icy mountain.

"You know what I mean. You have to grow up sometime, Kellen. You need to start earning more than you spend and make sound investments for the future. Better to learn that now when you have no one counting on you for support. God knows, you father didn't figure that out until it was too late."

"I'd say you landed on your feet," he'd responded.

All these years later, her second husband remained a source of friction between them.

She'd pursed her lips at the remark, causing half a dozen fine lines to feather around her mouth. They marred her otherwise youthful complexion. At sixty-two, Bess Faust Mackenzie remained a beautiful woman thanks to good genes, enviable bone structure and the skills of an expensive plastic surgeon.

"I did what was necessary. Meanwhile, you are content to blow through what little remains of the sizable inheritance from your grandfather. I'm surprised you've held on to the inn. It's prime real estate. Even in this soft market, the money would keep you comfortable for…well, for a few years anyway."

Kellen blocked out his mother's parting shot as he took a couple halting steps. She was right about a lot of things, but he would never sell the inn. In fact, he planned to take a far more active role in its oversight.

"Boss?"

He stopped and glanced over his shoulder, realizing he'd never answered Lou.

"Fine. Cell service can be a little spotty on the island, so be sure to leave a landline number."

"Will do." Lou offered a jaunty salute. He always seemed to be in a good mood. Same for Joe. Kellen used to be like that, too. As much as his mobility, he missed his old disposition.

"And Miss Wright?" he asked. "I assume she cleared out her belongings."

It was Joe who answered this time. "Yep. Brigit moved her clothes to the spare room, and her toiletries are in the guest bath now. Lou and I got all your stuff put away."

Kellen barely heard the last part. Brigit. First-name basis. Hmm. For a reason he couldn't fathom, he didn't like Joe's familiarity. Just as Brigit's laughter with the younger man had grated on his nerves earlier.

"The last I saw her, she was on the phone in her office." Lou chuckled. "It sounded like she was giving someone a chewing-out over a delivery snafu."

Formidable. No-nonsense. Take charge.

All of those descriptions applied, as did intelligent and capable, which foolishly he'd taken to mean she was dowdy, her looks nondescript. In Kellen's social circles, attractive women were vacuous and helpless—or at least they pretended to be. Draped in frumpy yellow vinyl Brigit had fit his preconceived notion perfectly. But once she'd peeled it off and had shoved the damp hair back from her face, well, Brigit Wright wasn't at all what he'd expected.

Kellen found her attractive, which was a surprise in itself. She wasn't anything like the women who usually caught his attention: flashy women whose beauty relied on a lot of enhancement, from hair extensions and capped teeth to serious breast augmentation.

Brigit was pretty in an understated way. She'd worn no makeup that he could see, although her dark lashes hadn't needed much help to highlight her blue eyes. Her hair was as black as coal. It hung past her shoulders in a limp curtain, lacking any discernable style. Of course, she had just been out for a walk in the rain.

What would she look like with her hair coiffed,

makeup accentuating her eyes and dressed up for a night out in something curve-hugging?

He silently answered himself with a second question. *What the hell does it matter?*

She was an employee. The same as Lou. The same as Joe. *Right.* Both his body and his mind mocked him.

He limped into the bedroom that had been his grandfather's during Kellen's childhood. It was decorated as differently as the lobby and the rest of the rooms. Bright, fresh, inviting even on this stormy afternoon. And more jars filled with shells on the bureau. The bedding had been turned down; the linens that peeked from beneath the comforter were creased in places, leaving little doubt that she had just changed the sheets for him.

He ran his fingers over the pillowcase. He would be sleeping in her bed.

And she would be in the room next door.

He swallowed hard and told himself the sudden uptick in his pulse rate was only because he was wondering how long the arrangement would have to continue. Weeks at least. Months? Possibly. She'd said the inn was booked, so it would be a while before a vacancy opened up.

Regardless, he had a lot to learn from the efficient Miss Wright if he hoped to run the resort as capably as she had been.

Eventually, that was his plan. He'd decided on it during his long stint in the hospital, when the shallowness of his life had been as impossible to ignore as his mounting debts. Kellen was done shirking all responsibility. Life as he'd known it was over in more ways than one.

In the meantime, he had an appointment with an orthopedic surgeon in Charleston the following week. He hoped to receive a better prognosis than the one the previous six had given him. *Hoped* being the operative word.

As if on cue, his leg muscles began to cramp and spasm. He leaned on the door frame to the bathroom to take the weight off his bad leg. When he glanced up, he spied the message. It was written in block letters on the mirror, and accompanied by an arrow that pointed to the bottle of over-the-counter painkillers on the counter.

"Non-habit-forming," he read aloud. "Take two and thank me later."

An odd sound echoed off the tile work as he studied his reflection. The hollowed-out eyes and gaunt cheeks no longer took him by surprise. But it came as a serious jolt to realize he was smiling. And that strange sound? It was his laughter.

CHAPTER THREE

A COUPLE HOURS LATER, Brigit was in the resort's commercial, galley-style kitchen helping the chef with dinner preparations when one of the swinging doors opened and her unwanted guest lumbered inside.

Sherry Crofton glanced up from the pot of sauce she was stirring on the cooktop.

"Sorry, but guests aren't allowed back here," the chef said politely, if firmly.

The kitchen was Sherry's domain, and she didn't care for outsiders breaching its door. To call her temperamental would be putting it mildly. She'd been known to shoo out the staff with a few choice words. One time, she'd even thrown a pot of blanched green beans at Danny's head when the young bellboy had had the audacity to filch a sugar cookie without asking.

But she was a damned fine chef, classically

trained with twenty years of experience running some of the finest kitchens on the East Coast. Brigit considered it a major coup that she'd managed to get Sherry to sign on as the chef at a small resort tucked away on an equally small island, regardless of the inn's growing reputation.

Kellen's brows notched up in surprise. It was a good bet he wasn't used to being told where he could and could not go, especially on property he owned.

Hoping to ward off a battle of the egos, Brigit set aside her paring knife and wiped her hands on the bib apron she'd donned to protect her clothes.

"I think we can make an exception for this one since he signs our paychecks."

"Mr. Faust?" the chef began, her tone brimming with disbelief. Her gaze slid to his leg and then over to the cane. "I didn't recognize you. You look—"

Sherry was known for her innovative dishes, but not so much for her tact. Brigit decided to keep the older woman from digging herself into a deeper a hole.

"Mr. Faust, this is Sherry Crofton, the inn's

chef. You're in for a treat at dinner tonight. She's making her specialty, pan-seared sea bass in an herbed butter sauce."

"Sounds excellent." He acknowledged the chef with a perfunctory nod, but his gaze strayed to Brigit and his eyes narrowed. "Why are you wearing an apron?"

"The sous chef is running late because of the storm. He lives on the mainland. I'm lending a hand with prep. Nothing that requires a culinary degree. Just chopping up vegetables for a steamed medley."

Eyes still narrowed, he asked, "Do you help out often?"

Since the question seemed rooted in genuine curiosity, she decided to answer truthfully. And, okay, she wanted him to be aware that she went above and beyond the call of duty when necessary.

"I wouldn't say often, but I pitch in when and where an extra pair of hands is needed, whether that's here in the kitchen or someplace else on the property."

Indeed, during her tenure, Brigit had changed

soiled bedding, flipped mattresses, unclogged drains and performed dozens of other less-than-glamorous chores. Nothing was beneath her, despite her high rank in the staff's pecking order. Apparently all of her predecessors had had other ideas. They'd deemed themselves too good for menial labor. Brigit figured her willingness to roll up her shirtsleeves was why she had earned the staff's respect as well as their loyalty. Turnover was at an all-time low.

Kellen rubbed his chin. "I see."

Did he? Unfortunately, she couldn't tell from his expression whether he thought this was a good use of her time and managerial skills or not. Some of her old insecurities bubbled to the surface.

You're so stupid, Brigit.

She banished her ex's hurtful words. She refused to start second-guessing herself again. Those days were long over.

Squaring her shoulders, she asked, "Was there something you needed?"

"Needed? No. Just…taking a look around. I

haven't been to the resort in years. A lot has changed."

From Kellen's tone, however, Brigit couldn't tell if he was happy about that or feeling nostalgic for the past.

His grandfather had owned the resort from the late 1950s on, which helped to explain why it was a virtual time capsule when she'd been hired. None of the managers before her had pressed for renovations to improve the business's bottom line. Perhaps they'd been as apathetic toward the place as their employer, seeing it as an easy paycheck rather than wanting to mine its potential. She'd gotten enough compliments from new guests as well as returning ones to know that the new look and amenities were a hit.

Speaking of changes, Kellen had undergone a bit of a transformation as well. His dark hair was wet as if he'd recently showered. He wore it slicked back from his forehead, although a few curls fell across his brow, giving him a rakish appeal. His face was freshly shaved, all shadow gone from its angular planes. But it wasn't the absence of stubble that caught her attention. It was the absence of a grimace.

"I see you took me up on the offer of some ibuprofen."

The barest hint of a smile lurked on his lips when he asked, "How do you know?"

"Well, for starters, you're no longer gritting your teeth."

"And?"

"You look…rested." The word *approachable* fit even better.

As did *handsome*. Despite his obvious weight loss, the man was definitely that. Instead of the workout attire he'd arrived wearing, he had on a crisp collared shirt that was tucked into a pair of beige dress pants. The carved wooden cane in his right hand added to his air of sophistication, although she was pretty sure he would take umbrage at her description.

"I got in a nap."

"And a workout?" Joe had mentioned something about that.

"No. I wasn't in the mood for more pain. Don't let Joe's baby face fool you. He can be ruthless."

Kellen's subtle attempt at humor came as a welcome surprise. She decided to return it.

"I would think that you'd pay him extra for that. No pain, no gain."

Just that quickly, his expression clouded. She gave an inaudible sigh. Apparently, she'd gone too far with the reminder of his slow recovery. While Brigit and Sherry traded covert shrugs, he looked away, breaking the silence a moment later when he asked, "New ovens, right?"

"Yes. The summer before last. And the cooktops were changed out at that time, too."

He glanced around, nodding.

Since it was so much easier to talk business than to try to exchange pleasantries, she continued. "The walk-in refrigerator just needed some repairs and it was good as new. Of course, your investment is almost fully paid back. Adding a meal package to the room rate has proved to be quite lucrative. And thanks to Sherry's talent we get quite a bit of non-guest traffic, too. The mayor stops by for Sunday brunch at least twice a month."

"Excellent." Kellen nodded, but she got the feeling he was only half listening to what she said.

Of course, she had sent him detailed reports every month. She'd like to think he'd read them.

"Are you hungry? Dinner service doesn't begin for another hour yet, but—"

"That's all right. Joe made me an omelet." He sent her a smile that bordered on sheepish. "We used up your eggs, by the way." He coughed. "And your bread. Joe was a little disappointed it wasn't whole wheat."

"Oh?" Brigit wasn't sure how she felt about strange men rummaging about in her cupboards. Every last inch of her private space had been invaded. But she kept her tone casual when she replied, "I'm sorry I don't keep more in my fridge and pantry. Sherry is such an excellent cook that I eat most of my meals here in the kitchen."

"In your office, you mean. The girl is a workhorse," Sherry told Kellen. Her expression turned shrewd when she added, "And probably due a raise."

Brigit smiled thinly. "Sherry and I will be heading to the mainland bright and early tomorrow for groceries and other supplies for the inn. We go the first and third Fridays of each month. If you give me a list, I'm happy to pick up whatever you need."

"I'll have Joe put something together. If you can't find everything, don't worry about it." Kellen's lip curled. "He likes to make wheatgrass shakes and other…healthy concoctions."

"The body is a temple?" she asked.

He snorted. "Mine feels more like an ancient ruin, but, yes, that's his philosophy."

Kellen looked away and his scowl returned in force. She didn't think it was their lighthearted banter that had irritated him. But something had. She followed the line of his vision to the far side of the room. The only thing there was Sherry's oversize calendar with the days that had already passed marked off with red *X*s.

"Is something wrong?" she asked.

He shook his head and, without another word, turned and limped out of the kitchen.

"Real friendly sort, isn't he?" Sherry muttered sarcastically once Kellen was out of earshot.

For a moment, a very brief moment, he had been.

Brigit returned to the cutting board and picked up her knife. "Let's just do our best to stay out of his way, okay? As fast as this summer is going, he'll be gone before we know it and things will be back to normal."

At least Brigit hoped that would be the case.

Kellen wasn't sure why seeing the days marked off on the kitchen calendar had torpedoed his mood. He only knew that where a moment earlier he had been close to joking, being hit with the reality that four months had passed since his accident had yanked the rug out from beneath him. The ibuprofen Brigit had put out for him had taken the edge off his physical pain. His emotional pain, however, was another matter.

Nothing seemed to dampen that.

Kellen wished it were nicer outdoors so that he could sit on the raised deck and watch the waves rise and swell. When he was a boy, the ocean had always had a calming effect on his emotions. Even on days such as this one, when the waves beat ruthlessly against the shore, at least he'd known what to expect. Waves would crash, but the water always receded and eventually calmed. Soon enough, the sun would come out and chase away the gloom, and the beach would be the same as it had been before the storm.

Nothing about his life now was consistent…except for his limp and the pain that came with it.

Guests milled about in the lobby, which was to be expected, he supposed, on such a wet, gloomy day. In the library, a couple of well-dressed women sat reading books in the sand colored wing chairs that flanked the French doors leading to another section of decking, and a few preppy-looking college kids huddled around the coffee table playing poker.

Kellen remembered playing cards in this very room as a boy. Gin rummy with his grandfather and sometimes with Herman, the old groundskeeper. Kellen had rarely won. When he had, he suspected it was because his grandfather had let him. The memory had him smiling, even as it made him sad.

God, he missed the old man. Hayden Faust had been the only doting adult in Kellen's life from age eleven on. After his father's death, his mother had been too busy looking for a new husband to pay him much mind. Then she'd remarried and, once again, Kellen had been shunted aside.

Even now Kellen refused to consider how desperate she must have felt to find her financial footing kicked out from under her. His grandfather, however, had cut her some slack.

During Kellen's final visit to the island, as they'd sat in this very room, Hayden had told him, "I'm not condoning the way your mother has treated you since remarrying, but try to see things from her perspective."

"What do you mean?" he'd asked.

"You're so much like your father."

"You say that as if it's a bad thing." Kellen had laughed, not sure how else to respond.

His grandfather hadn't cracked so much as a smile as he'd laid his weathered hand on Kellen's shoulder.

"I loved my son dearly, but I'm not blind to his shortcomings. He made some poor choices over the years. Choices that your mother has paid for in more ways than one."

"What are you saying?"

"I'm saying, be sure you make better ones. Make me proud, Kellen."

A final request that Kellen had failed to honor. What would his grandfather think of the choices he'd made now? The likely answer had Kellen limping back to the privacy of his rooms.

"Mr. F?" Joe poked his head around the door.

Although Kellen was awake, he kept his eyes closed and feigned sleep. He'd been lying on the bed in his room for the past two hours thinking and trying to work out the details of his plan B. A plan that Brigit Wright wasn't going to like when he eventually told her about it.

His grandfather had left Kellen the inn with the hope he would actually run it, rather than merely sign checks and authorize improvements when he took a break from the ski slopes in Europe.

It was time to start making those better choices the older man had urged.

"Boss?" Joe called again.

Leave me alone! Kellen shouted the words in his head, but he didn't say them out loud. He was tired of being sullen and disagreeable, even as he felt powerless to change his mood. So he kept his eyes closed and his breathing deep and even. He expected that would be the end of it. Joe would go away and Kellen could continue to stew in silence.

But his physical therapist wasn't alone.

"He's sleeping soundly," Kellen heard Joe tell whoever was with him. "Just go in and grab what you need."

"I'd hate to disturb him." Brigit's voice.

She sounded indecisive. Once again Kellen found himself wanting to shout, *Leave!* His reason this time was embarrassment.

Could she see him? God, he hoped not. When he'd returned to the room, he'd shucked off his other clothes and now lay atop the comforter wearing a pair of black nylon gym shorts. Briefly, he'd pulled on a T-shirt whose neon green slogan was intended to inspire. Since it only served to mock him in his current condition, he'd tugged it off as well. He'd balled it up and tossed it. It was on the floor somewhere across the room. He'd never been embarrassed to go shirtless before, but these days he was a pale imitation of the physically fit man he'd been. Still, it would be the lesser of two evils if her gaze remained on his chest and didn't detour to the ugly web of scars on his mangled leg.

"Perhaps I'll come back later," she said.

"You'd rather see him when he's awake?" Joe's tone was wry and teasing.

Brigit chuckled and Kellen bristled inwardly. He didn't appreciate being the butt of their joke.

"You make a good point," she said. "Okay. I'm going in. I'll be quiet so as not to disturb him."

"I know you will." This time Joe chuckled. "Hey, I'm going to make wheatgrass smoothies. Stop by the kitchen on your way out. I'll make one for you."

"A wheatgrass smoothie?"

"They're delicious and good for you."

"Sure. Can't wait."

Liar, Kellen thought.

Footsteps sounded then. Joe leaving? Where was Brigit? Kellen strained his ears, listening for the creak of floorboards or the rustle of fabric—anything to announce that she was moving about inside the bedroom. Finally, on the opposite side of the room from the hallway, he heard a door squeak. The bathroom? The closet? He chanced opening his eyes. The room was dim thanks to the pulled shades. It wasn't quite dusk outside, although the weather certainly made it seem later. Brigit was in the walk-in closet, standing under the light. He studied her profile as she rose up on her toes and pulled down a basket from the one of the shelves.

She was slender and pretty in a way that left him to wonder if she purposefully downplayed her looks. After she gathered whatever it was that she'd come in to get, she turned. Through slit eyes, Kellen watched her switch off the light and gently close the closet.

She started to tiptoe toward the bedroom door, but then stopped at the foot of the bed. If she had looked at his face, she would have realized he was awake. His eyes were fully open now. But she wasn't looking at his face or any other part of his anatomy found above the waist. She was studying his bad leg, starting at the ankle. The break had healed, but the not the damage. The calf was noticeably smaller than its counterpart on his good leg. Joe attributed the disparity to muscle atrophy, although he couldn't guarantee Kellen that regular workouts would fix that.

Her gaze wandered up to his knee before skimming his thigh. It wasn't a pretty sight, to be sure. Nothing could be done to erase the scars from where jagged bone had ripped through his flesh or the multiple surgeries that had followed.

She didn't strike him as the squeamish sort, but she closed her eyes briefly. Did he disgust her? Did she pity him? He wasn't sure which reaction would be worse. He only knew he could tolerate no more of her thorough examination.

"Seen enough?"

She nearly dropped the belt she's retrieved from the closet.

"You startled me."

Spoiling for a fight, he levered up on one elbow. "You didn't answer my question."

"I didn't mean to stare. I was…I was just…"

"Curious?" he demanded.

She cleared her throat. Even in the dim light, he could tell she was flustered and probably blushing. Embarrassed? Definitely. But not turned on. Why would she be? He was an invalid, repulsive. Angry with them both, he spat out in a suggestive tone, "My leg might be mangled, but I can assure you, everything else is in working order."

She did drop the belt now, and her hand flew to her chest. "Excuse me?"

"I think you heard me."

At that, he expected her to stomp out of the room in a huff. He should have known his dot-every-i and cross-every-t manager would do no such thing. Indeed, Brigit drew closer and came around the side of the bed.

"I heard you. I was trying to give you the benefit of the doubt."

"And now you expect me to apologize," he said, keeping his tone insolent.

"As a matter of fact…" She fisted her hands, settled them on her hips and sent him an arched look.

Nice hips. Not too wide, not too narrow. Neatly rounded, and along with her firm backside, just right. Given Kellen's position on the bed, the hips he was admiring were practically at eye level. His mouth watered and parts of his body that had been dormant for months began to stir back to life. Some of his frustration and anger dissipated, only to be replaced by feelings that were far more dangerous.

Even though he knew he was playing with fire, Kellen was helpless to keep his gaze from traveling up Brigit's slender frame and touching on all of the parts that interested him.

"Well?" she demanded.

Their gazes met, collided really. He didn't see sparks fly, but he swore he felt them. They showered his skin. The sensation was life-affirming. He reveled in it.

Common sense took a backseat to desire, and he taunted, "You first."

"What?"

"You apologize first."

"You expect *me* to apologize to you?"

Her tone hovered between incredulous and royally ticked off. Perversely, he found it a turn-on. As he did her narrowed eyes and pinched lips.

"That's right."

"What am I to apologize for?" she demanded.

"Well, for starters, you're trespassing. You're in my bedroom…uninvited." *A small matter that could be remedied easily enough*, his libido whispered before he could quiet it.

"This is…well, until this afternoon, it was my bedroom. I'm hardly trespassing."

He held up a finger. "Technically, as the resort's owner—"

She'd worked up a good head of steam and talked over his clarification of the bedroom's ownership.

"Look, I just came in to get a belt from the closet. I would have asked *permission*—" her lips twisted on the word "—but you were sleeping and I didn't want to disturb you. The fact is, I wasn't given much time to gather up my belongings before you moved in. If you want an apology for that, fine. I'm *so sorry* for the inconvenience."

She didn't sound sorry. She sounded aggrieved, irritated and ready to combust. Kellen knew he should quit provoking her, but he couldn't help himself. He pressed.

"You got your belt, yet here you stand, Miss Wright. Er, Brigit. Under the circumstances I think we should be on a first-name basis. Don't you?"

"I...I..." she sputtered, glaring at him as if he'd grown a second head.

"You're standing at my bedside. And you were staring at me."

"I wasn't staring—"

"You were. Or maybe I should say gawking. The way one does at a train wreck."

Kellen pushed all the way to a sitting position. The instant he did so, excruciating pain radiated out from his knee, shooting down to his ankle and up to his hip. He wasn't able to bite back his yelp. Apparently, the ibuprofen had worn off.

"Mr. Faust?" She started forward.

"It's Kellen, dammit. Kellen!" he spat, still

angry with both of them. Indeed, in that instant, he was back to being angry with everyone and everything. His new status quo. "Just go."

"Do you need—"

"Do you really want to know what I need, Brigit?" When she stood there eyeing him, he prompted, "Well, do you?"

"I know what you need." She said it softly, a hint of a smile playing on her lips.

Despite his anger and the raw pain he was experiencing, that Mona Lisa smile tugged at places inside him.

"Tell me."

"A wheatgrass smoothie. I'll have Joe bring one in. I hear they're delicious and good for you." She turned on her heel and walked out with her shoulders squared, her chin up.

Kellen flopped back on the bed. Anger dissipated along with the worst of the pain. Shame and embarrassment settled in their place. He wondered what it said about him that the most alive he'd felt in months had been while provoking an employee.

Brigit was right about one thing. He was the one who owed her an apology.

CHAPTER FOUR

BRIGIT WAS FUMING. Molars grinding, she stomped out of the apartment without saying a word to Joe. The blender was on high, making it easier to just wave and go. Anger carried her all the way to the resort's kitchen. Although dinner service was over, she asked Sherry, "Got anything for me to chop into very small pieces?"

The cook eyed her knowingly. "Something tells me it would be a bad idea to hand you a sharp knife right now. What's got you so upset, anyway?"

"Not what. Who."

Kellen Faust.

Who did the man think he was, demanding that Brigit apologize for being in her own bedroom? She didn't give a damn if he owned the resort. The room, the entire apartment, was hers or it had been until just that morning. The man was acting like an inconsiderate tyrant.

One with a faulty memory to boot.

He'd agreed with her plan to turn the old manager's quarters into a luxury suite for high-end guests. He'd agreed to let her move into the unused owner's apartment. She had saved their written correspondence to that effect. Maybe she should remind him. Maybe she should pull out her contract, which clearly stated that she was entitled to on-site accommodations as part of her compensation, and return to the bedroom and confront him.

She swallowed, thinking of the sight of the man lying on her bed. Okay, so she'd glanced at him on her way back to the door. Maybe she'd stared for a couple seconds longer than was polite. Fine, she'd outright ogled him, which definitely was not her style. But Kellen Faust sans shirt and wearing shorts, well, he'd certainly caught her attention. And since she'd thought he was asleep, she'd figured it wouldn't hurt to satisfy her curiosity and snatch a closer look.

She'd gotten an eyeful, all right. The accident had taken a toll on his once-fit body. Even allowing for the fact that photographs added weight,

Kellen was definitely thinner now, even more so than he'd initially appeared when fully dressed. He wasn't skinny exactly. Lean, wiry—those descriptions would be more accurate. Regardless, he was all male, and seeing his bare limbs, scarred or not, spread out on her comforter had had an unsettling effect on her breathing.

Brigit tried to recall how long had it been since she'd felt the air back up in her lungs where a man was concerned. Or that tightening sensation low in her belly. She couldn't. Within the first year of her marriage, things had gone from acceptable to bad. From there, they'd made the leap to god-awful. In all, four years of her life wasted. It still shamed her to admit that she'd allowed herself to be a doormat for that length of time.

In the immediate aftermath of her ugly divorce, she'd been too shell-shocked even to think of dating again. Once she'd landed the job at the resort, she'd been happy to focus on her career. It wasn't that she didn't have time for men. She didn't *make* time. While staring at Kellen, Brigit had begun to have second thoughts.

Stupid, stupid, stupid. Standing in the kitchen now, she rubbed her temples.

"I think I can guess who you mean," Sherry said, pulling Brigit from her introspection.

Be that as it may, a good manager didn't gossip, much less talk disrespectfully about the boss, so Brigit shook her head and worked up what she hoped passed for a smile.

"I'm just frustrated with one of our suppliers," she lied. "He keeps trying to jack up the prices we've already agreed to."

"Supplier, hmm?" Sherry didn't look fooled.

Brigit cleared her throat. "Thanks for letting me vent. I'll just get out of your way."

It was after eleven o'clock when Brigit finally returned to the apartment that night. Joe was sitting on the couch watching television. Kellen, thankfully, was nowhere to be seen. She let out a breath she hadn't been aware she was holding and smiled at the physical therapist.

"I hope you weren't waiting up on my account." She grimaced then. "I never got your bedding."

"That's okay." Joe cocked his head sideways. "Everything all right?"

"Fine." She shrugged. "Why do you ask?"

"You left in a hurry earlier, and you've been gone ever since. I thought maybe Mr. F had woken up while you were in the room and said something to upset you."

Oh, Kellen had said something, all right. Something off-color and out of line. Something that had made her blood boil, but not only with temper. As such, she wasn't going to share the details with Joe. So she waved a hand.

"I had some work to finish up."

She swore her bogus explanation received the same knowing look from Joe that her earlier fabrication about supplier trouble had received from Sherry. Brigit went to grab bedding and an extra pillow from the linen closet. When she returned, Joe had turned off the television and was moving the coffee table so he could pull out the sofa bed.

"I got this," he said when she tried to help him. Then he went on as if she'd asked about their mutual employer. "Mr. F was in a lousy mood tonight."

"Oh?"

The bed unfolded, the mattress flopping down on the frame with an unceremonious *plop*. Her thoughts were on another mattress. Another man.

Joe said, "He complained about his leg bothering him."

"The ibuprofen probably wore off. He needs to take two tablets every four to six hours, according to the dosage instructions on the bottle."

Joe pulled the fitted bottom sheet around the top corner of the mattress. "He brought some of the pain on himself. He spent too much time today sitting or lying down. He blew off our afternoon therapy session. He needs to keep moving, despite the pain. The scar tissue needs to be stretched along with his tendons. The longer he stays stationary, the stiffer his muscles become."

His muscles weren't the only part of his anatomy that had become rigid. Brigit swallowed and focused her attention on securing her ends of the fitted sheet.

Kellen slept poorly, tossing and turning—and then groaning in pain—for the better part of the night. His conscience bothered him as much as his leg. Maybe even more since he'd grown used to the nagging physical ache.

He'd heard Brigit come into the apartment the previous night. She'd talked with Joe for a bit, although he hadn't been able to hear the actual words of their conversation. Afterward, her steps had been light in the hallway before she'd entered the spare room. He'd pictured her curled up on the uncomfortable futon, and his conscience had nipped at him again, not because he'd displaced her from her bed, but because his imagination had worked overtime on what she'd been wearing.

He tossed back the covers now. He needed to apologize. He'd leave out his wayward imagination, though, and concentrate on his rude behavior from the day before.

He found her on the private deck off the living room. She was seated in one of the lounge chairs, her fingers busily clicking over the keys of a laptop computer. A mug of something hot was on a small table next to her. Joe was at the rail drinking an unsightly green concoction through a straw. He spied Kellen through the sliding glass door and rushed over to open it.

"Good morning, Mr. F!" he said with his usual good cheer. "You're up early. Brigit and I were just out here enjoying the sunrise. It's going to be a great day."

The man's enthusiasm should have been contagious. Kellen glanced at Brigit, who looked as unmotivated as he felt.

"Want a wheatgrass smoothie?"

What Kellen wanted was a cup of high-octane coffee and a couple extra-strength ibuprofen. But he needed a few minutes alone with Brigit, and Joe had just provided him the perfect excuse.

"Yes."

Kellen's response not only had Joe's eyes widening; Brigit turned from her typing to look at him.

"Really?" Joe said.

"You're always touting their health benefits."

"I didn't think you were listening," the younger man replied with comical honestly.

"I'll also take a couple painkillers and some coffee when you get a chance."

Joe grinned. "Coming right up. Anything for you, Brigit?"

She shook her head. "I'm good."

Once they were alone, Kellen moved to the lounge chair next to hers. Its low height would make sitting down difficult. Bearing his weight on the cane, he tried to lower himself slowly, but his leg gave out halfway down and he landed on the seat with a *plop*. Getting up without assistance would be impossible. He decided not to think about that now and tucked the cane under the chair.

"I'd offer to help, but I know you don't want it," she remarked as he struggled to get both of his legs up on the footrest.

He grunted and surprised them both by admitting, "It's damned depressing to need assistance to perform something as simple as taking a seat."

She studied him a moment before nodding. Then she went back to her typing.

He tried again. "It's a nice morning. The calm after the storm."

She nodded again, this time without looking up from her laptop. A spreadsheet was open in one of the windows on the screen. Some sort of chart that compared the previous year's energy costs to this one's. In another window was an article on solar panels, to which she was adding notes. It was not even 6:00 a.m. and Brigit was already showered, dressed and on the clock. Most of the women he knew would have been a few hours into their beauty sleep after a late night out partying.

He cleared his throat, but the words still stuck a little before finally coming out. "I…I wanted to talk to you, Brigit."

"Brigit, is it? We're sitting on the deck. Should we still be on a first-name basis?" she asked nonchalantly.

Meanwhile—*tap-tap-tap*—the fingers on the keyboard never slowed.

Kellen scratched a hand over the stubble on his jaw. He deserved that. "I owe you an apology for what I said and for how I acted yesterday."

Tap-tap-tap. "Yes. You do." Her tone was matter-of-fact.

"Could you…could you maybe stop typing for a minute and look at me?"

She hit a few more keys, exhaled slowly and then closed the laptop. Turning in her seat, she gave him her full attention. He almost wished she hadn't. Bright blue eyes fringed with amazingly long black lashes left him feeling laid bare.

"I am sorry. The way I acted…the things I said…I was out of line."

"Apology accepted. Thank you." She lifted a hand and her fingers caught in the ends of her dark hair, twirling some of it in a gesture that struck him as almost tentative. "I should have waited to get my belt."

"You left it on the floor, by the way."

"I know."

He reached into the pocket of his track pants and pulled out the slim length of leather, which he'd wound into a tight coil. "Here."

A smile tugged at her lips. "Thanks."

"We got off on the wrong foot." He snorted at his unintentionally apropos phrasing. Since humbling himself wasn't as difficult as he'd presumed it to be, he continued, "I should have realized that my early arrival here would cause some…upheaval."

Early or otherwise, it had and then some, especially for the woman sitting beside him.

"Can I ask you something?" she said after a moment.

"Sure. What?"

"Did you even read the monthly reports I've been sending for the past five years?"

The woman certainly didn't pull any punches. He decided he owed her the truth. "No. I glanced at them. Well, some of them, but…no. I didn't give any a thorough reading."

"So when you approved my ideas and gave the green light to my renovation plans, you did so blindly?"

Her tone held a note of censure. Or was it disappointment? His stomach took a surprising roll. It had been a long time since Kellen had cared what someone thought of him. Not since his grandfather.

"My schedule was pretty busy." He laughed without humor and came clean. "All those parties, you know."

"I wouldn't know. I work for living, even on the weekends."

Oh, yeah. Definitely censure.

"I should have read them." A responsible business owner would have, he admitted to himself. "But I did and I still do trust your judgment. Besides, we graduated from the same business school."

"*You* have a degree from the University of Connecticut?"

The shock on her face was unmistakable and reflected in the disbelief in her tone. Kellen's battered ego took another blow.

"I haven't put it to much use, but yes, I have a degree from UConn, earned a few years before you would have started classes. When I interviewed you for the job—" which he'd done by phone and email between runs down the slopes in the alpine town of Grindelwald "—I was impressed by your credentials, even if you didn't have much practical experience."

Her expression turned oddly guarded and she glanced away.

"I got married right after graduation." She paused. "My husband didn't think I needed to work."

"You're married?" That came as a surprise. An unpleasant one based on the way his stomach somersaulted. Why would it matter if she was taken? Kellen rallied as quickly as he could, hoping that none of his dismay showed in his expression. He was her employer. As such, her marital status was none of his business, legally or otherwise. That was why it hadn't come up during the interview process or any of their other dealings.

"Happily divorced," she corrected. Her jaw clenched after she said it and she reached for her coffee cup.

It wasn't relief he felt, he told himself. That would be inappropriate. Still, he couldn't help but be intrigued. Not only about what had happened to end Brigit's marriage, but what kind of man this quietly attractive and obviously smart woman would have wed in the first place. But he kept his questions to himself. Business, he reminded himself. That was the basis of their relationship. And when it came to business, in spite of the degree he'd earned more than a decade earlier, Kellen had a lot to learn.

Thinking of that, he noted, "None of the three

managers before you thought to implement any capital improvements."

More damning, Kellen had never thought to implement any either. The inn was his inheritance, yet he'd all but left it to rot while he'd done his damnedest to confirm his mother's low of opinion of him as a wastrel.

Brigit was no longer clenching her jaw. In fact, he heard excitement bubble in her voice and saw it spark in her eyes as she told him, "I saw so much potential for change the first time I toured the property. This location is amazing. The oceanfront view…." She motioned to the horizon where the sun blazed gold and orange before blurring into pastel shades of pink and blue.

"It should have been packed year-round. Yet it had vacancies during the peak tourist season. And the internet reviews were dismal. People want amenities. When they go on vacation, they are willing to pay for six-hundred-thread-count sheets, complimentary turndown service complete with mints on their pillows, satellite television and wireless internet. Give them the option of superb dining on-site and they will not only book a weekend, they'll come back again and recommend us to their friends."

"Your changes have made sure of that. I may not have read every line of your reports and correspondence, but that much I figured out."

The compliment had her blinking, but she said dryly, "I would imagine the bottom line speaks for itself."

He nodded. "It speaks volumes. Revenues are up—what?—two, two hundred and fifty percent from five years ago?"

"Three hundred," she amended after a discreet cough. Though her expression remained neutral, he saw pride spark in her eyes. And no wonder.

She'd tripled his income. At this rate, the money he'd invested in upgrades would be repaid in no time. His future was secure, financially at least.

And he owed it all to her.

Guilt throbbed like a bad tooth since his newly worked out plan ultimately would see her displaced from her job. After all, he doubted someone of Brigit's caliber would want to stay on in a reduced capacity, basically sharing managerial duties with him once Kellen was sufficiently healed and up to speed. He'd offer her the option, of course. He wasn't a fool. As much as he wanted to take over, he didn't plan to work around the clock like she apparently did.

If she left—more likely when—he would see to it that she was fairly compensated. He made a mental note to meet with his lawyer to draft a generous severance package when he went into Charleston for his doctor appointment.

"Thank you. For everything," he told her now.

Then he reached over and laid one of his hands over hers. The gesture was intended to be companionable, but the way his body responded to the benign contact was far baser in nature. Her skin was soft, warm.

She pulled her hand away, using it to tuck a few stray strands of dark hair behind her ear. Her cheeks had turned a becoming shade of pink, and he couldn't help wondering if it was the contact that had thrown her or his gratitude.

Finally, she replied, "The Christmas bonus I received was thanks enough." She picked up her coffee cup then and focused her attention on its contents. "I like living here. On the island, at the resort. And I like this job. I'm *good* at it."

He found the comment odd. She seemed to be trying to convince him of her competence. If so, she needn't have bothered.

While he covertly studied Brigit's profile, wondering what beyond job satisfaction drove her to labor for such long hours, she sipped her coffee and scanned the horizon. She had a nice profile. He took in the slope of her cheek, slight lift of her nose, delicate jaw that ended in a blunt chin. All of it stirred him up in a way he found both compelling and concerning. The squawk of gulls and slap of waves on sand were the only sounds to break the silence until the door opened and Joe stepped out onto the deck. He carried a tray that held a mug of coffee and a glass filled with a sickly looking green concoction that had Kellen's taste buds staging a revolt.

"Here you go, Mr. F. One wheatgrass smoothie as requested. I took the liberty of adding half a banana." The young man grinned. "They're an excellent source of potassium."

"Mmm." Kellen grimaced and his gag reflex

threatened to kick in. He hated bananas almost as much as he hated wheatgrass.

"Well, I need to get ready to meet Sherry to go shopping on the mainland. I have your list," Brigit told Joe. Then she rose to her feet, laptop in hand, her gaze on Kellen. "Enjoy your smoothie."

Was it his imagination or was she biting back a grin?

CHAPTER FIVE

KELLEN WOKE EARLY the following Wednesday morning. Even earlier than he had been waking for the past several days. He used to sleep till noon. Even after his accident, he hadn't become an early riser, rousing by ten o'clock but only because that was when Joe scheduled his first session.

Since his arrival at Faust Haven the week before, however, he'd been up each day by dawn. Being on Hadley Island seemed to have reset his internal clock. He didn't mind. He'd felt more rested the past few days than he had during the past several months.

This morning, however, he couldn't claim to feel the same. That was because today was *the* day. His doctor appointment loomed at one o'clock. Kellen had slept fitfully when he'd slept at all. What would the specialist in Charleston say?

He didn't want to believe that nothing more could be done, that his current physical condition, with its accompanying limp and many limitations, was the best he could hope for when it came to his recovery. But it was a very good possibility that this doctor would tell him the same thing all of the other doctors had. The same suffocating sense of defeat that had defined his life for the past four months settled over him.

After lying in bed for an hour, his mind racing as much as it wandered, he finally threw back the covers, rolled to his side and struggled out of bed. His leg was stiff, sore. It always was first thing in the morning. He performed a few of the stretching exercises Joe recommended and got dressed in his usual outfit of loose-fitting track pants and a lightweight T-shirt.

Dawn had chased the darkness from the apartment by the time he stepped into the hallway. As he passed the guest room, he noticed that the door was ajar. He glanced inside, doubting even as he did so that he would find Brigit there.

At this hour, she would be out on the deck, a mug of coffee on the table at her side and the computer booted up and open on her lap. It was how she started her days, a routine that she apparently followed seven mornings a week unless the weather was bad. So, for the past week, coffee on the deck was how Kellen had started his as well.

He couldn't tell if his presence bothered her, although if it did, he suspected she would have found a different spot. The resort had other decks, although none quite as private as the one off the owner's apartment.

They sat, sipping their coffee and watching the sunrise. She'd pay bills or perform some other task related to the resort. All the while he would ask questions, the kind with answers a conscientious owner already would know.

Kellen hadn't been a conscientious owner. Both he and Brigit knew that. He gave her credit for refraining from saying so. Still, he'd caught her questioning expression whenever he made an inquiry. As patient as she was in answering, he figured she also had to be annoyed.

What did it say about him, Kellen wondered, that he found the furrow that formed between her amazing eyes whenever she was confused or agitated to be so sexy?

Movement inside the room caught his notice. Not only was Brigit there, she was…undressing. He should look away. He should go away. But he stood rooted in place, gaze glued to her slim figure. Her back was to him, but he caught a glimpse of sky-blue lace stretched across the pale skin of her spine as she pulled off the shirt she'd been wearing and traded it for another. Her movements were practical and precise, hardly the sort choreographed to seduce. Still, the sight of smooth ivory skin and lean contours had his mouth going dry, and for one ridiculous moment Kellen found it difficult to breathe.

He managed to inhale, and a familiar and all too pleasing smell filled his nose. Clean and crisp with a hint of citrus. It was the same fragrance that teased him at night while he lay in her bed. The sheets might have been fresh, but her scent was all around him. Making him yearn. Making him burn. That heat enveloped him now, threatened to incinerate what remained of his manners. He took a couple of halting steps backward and cleared his throat noisily in an effort to announce his presence. When he drew even with the door a second time, Brigit was pulling it fully open.

"Good morning," she said.

"Good morning."

She'd exchanged the blue shirt she usually wore for a turquoise version in a similar cut. Both had the inn's logo embroidered on the chest and… he was staring at her breasts. He ripped his gaze away only to have it settle on the tangle of sheets that littered the futon behind her. He frowned.

"That doesn't look very comfortable," he murmured.

Brigit glanced over her shoulder. "Not as comfortable as the queen-size pillow top you're sleeping on," she agreed. "But it's not so bad."

"No?" He thought it looked like a medieval torture device.

He grimaced. "I've never apologized for the inconvenience my stay has caused you."

Her eyes widened fractionally, but that was

the only sign his words surprised her. "No, you haven't."

"I am sorry, Brigit."

She nodded. "It's all right."

But it wasn't. His thoughtlessness made him ashamed. "I should take the guest room. I can have Joe move my things in here today, and you can have your room back."

"I appreciate the offer, but it really is *your* room. Besides, you wouldn't be comfortable on the futon." She motioned over her shoulder at the piece of furniture under discussion. "It sits too low to the ground."

It was like the lounge chair on the deck in that regard. And they both knew how much effort it took for Kellen to get up from it.

Brigit was saying, "My back will survive the inconvenience. It's not like it's forever."

No, indeed. It wouldn't be forever. Eventually, their living arrangements, along with their business arrangement, would be decided. But only one of them knew that at the moment. He changed the subject. "I thought you'd already be out on the deck. It's after six."

"I was, but I spilled some coffee on my shirt."

"So, that's why you changed it." He realized his faux pas even before her eyes narrowed. "I mean, so you came into change it."

"How long have you been up?" she asked.

"Up or awake?" He shrugged and surprised himself by admitting, "I didn't get much sleep last night."

"You have a doctor's appointment today, right? Joe mentioned it."

Her gaze lowered momentarily to the cane gripped in his hand. It was what everyone saw when they looked at him, part and parcel of that all-important first impression.

"Right." And an appointment with his attorney, Kellen added silently.

As much as he would prefer Brigit stay on in some capacity, he doubted someone as adept in making decisions and giving orders in the day-to-day running of the resort, would be willing to follow his. He would ask her to stay, but he also would offer her a generous severance package and glowing letter of recommendation to help with her job search in the more likely event that she decided to go.

"I'll have my fingers crossed for you."

"Thanks." He frowned at the cane. "I'm hoping for a more promising prognosis." Again, his admission surprised him. What was it about Brigit that made it so easy to bare his soul?

"And if you don't get it? What then?"

Kellen squinted at her. "You know, you're the first person who's asked me that."

He didn't count his mother. After all, she hadn't asked. She'd told Kellen what he needed to do: grow up.

Brigit glanced away. "I'm sorry. I shouldn't have—"

"No. I appreciate your bluntness in this case." He took a deep breath and exhaled slowly. "To be honest, I don't know what I'll do. This is the sixth specialist. At what point do I just…"

Give up. His fingers tightened on the cane's handle until his knuckles turned white. He was unable to go on.

"Joe says you don't always do your exercises.

You can't expect to recover fully if you don't put in the effort."

"Recover fully." He made a scoffing noise.

She wasn't deterred. "All right. Recover more of your lost mobility. That is the reason behind rehab, isn't it?"

No one else had dared to say such things to him.

Even Joe trod lightly when it came to admonishing Kellen for his lack of effort. Instead of making him want to tell her to go to hell, her straightforward nature compelled him to reply with similar honesty. "Yes, that is the reason behind rehab, but...but some days it's all I can do to get out of bed. Some days everything seems so...so...damned pointless."

The admission hung between them, suspended in the ensuing silence. Something flickered in her eyes. Understanding? Empathy?

"That's depression talking. It makes every obstacle seem insurmountable," she said after a moment. Her tone was filled with compassion, which only made it worse.

Depression? As if he weren't already feeling

helpless and emasculated. Pride had him snapping, "What, are you a shrink now?"

She appeared to take his irritable tone in stride. "No. I just know that when a person is at his or her lowest point, it's not always easy to grab the nearest rope, even when it's well within reach."

"The voice of experience?"

She eyed him for a moment before speaking again.

"I'm heading back out to the deck. I have a few more emails to send before I get to work. Are you coming?"

Her switch in topics made it clear she knew something about how difficult it was to climb one's way back up after hitting rock bottom. Her divorce? That seemed the obvious culprit, but he let the matter drop.

"Can I get a cup of coffee?" he asked.

"Sure. I'll even carry it outside for you," she offered with a smile that seemed more friendly than merely polite. He decided to think of that as progress.

Kellen followed her. His pace was slow and measured compared to her brisk one, and far less graceful. The view was worth it, though. Well worth it, he thought, as his gaze dipped south to watch her hips swing side to side. Although her movements were economical, that didn't keep them from being sexy. His interest was piqued again.

When they reached the living room, he glanced toward the sofa. The bed had been folded back up, cushions and throw pillows returned to their original positions.

"Is Joe out on the deck already?"

"No. He went for a run. He left about forty minutes ago, so he should be back within the hour. I'm sure he'll be happy to whip up one of his smoothies for you then."

Kellen groaned. "That's what I'm afraid of."

She stopped at the granite-topped island that separated the kitchen from the living room and poured their coffee before starting for the door that led to the deck.

It was breezier this morning than it had been on previous days. The wind caught at her hair and pushed several ribbons of it across her face. She finger-combed them back into place after depositing their coffee on a table and settling onto her lounge chair. His fingers itched to do the task for her, itched to touch her hair. He wouldn't find it sticky with gels or sprays. But soft, silky…

He concentrated on getting onto his chair. He'd gotten better at it over the past week, but it still required more effort than it should. As for getting up, well, he couldn't do that unless he positioned the lounge chair next to the deck's railing, which he used to haul himself to his feet.

By the time Kellen had his legs stretched out in front of him, Brigit was already tapping away on the computer's keyboard.

Emails, she'd said. He assumed they were business-related, since, from what he could tell, the woman was on the clock 24/7.

What drove her? While he appreciated her above-and-beyond approach to her duties, it wasn't expected. Nor was it particularly healthy. He nearly chuckled aloud at that. As if he had any right to judge another person's lifestyle.

He glanced idly at the computer screen, expecting to see her confirming reservations or responding to guests' suggestions on the internet comment board. Too late, he realized the message she was writing was personal.

"Do you always read other people's correspondence?" she inquired blandly

Despite his embarrassment, he marveled again at how appealing he found her bluntness.

"No. Sorry. I just assumed that whatever you were working on was business-related."

"I do have a life." She glanced over at him in seeming challenge.

Not as much of one as she should, but he kept the opinion to himself. He did ask, "Who's Will?"

Her former husband? A current lover? Kellen found neither possibility palatable.

She closed the laptop and gave him her full attention, blue eyes blazing bright with an emotion he couldn't pinpoint. He didn't expect her to answer, but she said, "He's my nephew."

"Lucky you." When she frowned, he added, "I'm an only child. No siblings, no nieces or nephews. Just…me."

With his father and his grandfather gone and his mother estranged, that was truly the case.

"I have a sister. Robbie. Short for Roberta.

She's older by eighteen months." Her expression softened, and the hint of a smile lurked around the corners of her mouth.

"You're close."

"Yes." Now she frowned again. "We don't see each other as often as we'd like. She lives in Pennsylvania."

"Does Will have siblings?"

"No. My sister wanted more children, but Mitchell, my brother-in-law, he…he was a Marine."

Was. Her use of the past tense had his stomach dropping. "God, I'm sorry. Iraq?"

"Afghanistan. A roadside bomb took out half his patrol. Will was a toddler at the time. He doesn't have any real memories of his dad."

"Sorry," Kellen said again, although the word seemed grossly inadequate under the circumstances. Her family had lost someone to the violencc of war. In some ways, it made Kellen's own struggles seem minor, especially since his accident had been the result of foolish hot-dogging to meet a dare rather than something as honorable as serving his country. It was a humbling realization.

She was saying, "Will is eight now. For the past couple of summers, he and my sister have come out to Hadley Island over the Fourth of July for a visit. There's always a big fireworks display in Charleston that's visible from the western shore. We spread out a blanket, bring a basket of snacks and watch it."

"So they'll be coming this summer?" he asked, oddly envious of the picture of domestic bliss her words had helped conjure up.

"They stay with me, Kellen," she replied.

Despite the pointed look that accompanied her words, it took him a moment to realize what she meant.

Then, "Ah. Got it. No room at the inn and no room in your apartment. I'm s—"

"Don't apologize. What's done is done. I've promised Will that he and his mom can come another time later in the year, maybe during Christmas break."

The assumption being that Kellen wouldn't be at Faust Haven then. He swallowed. He wasn't planning on going anywhere. But would Brigit still be on his payroll at Christmas? Or would she have moved on to manage another resort?

While she went back to her typing, he scanned their surroundings. White-capped waves danced on the horizon before crashing to shore. Down the beach, he caught a glimpse of Joe. For a physically fit young man, he looked winded and pained. Still, Kellen envied him.

"I used to run every day," he remarked almost to himself.

Brigit looked up from the computer screen. "You're a runner?"

Was. But he nodded without bothering to correct her, and said, "I ran five miles every other day when I was skiing. Every day when I wasn't." He pointed in the direction of his physical therapist. "I'd like to think I didn't look as miserable as Joe does right now."

Brigit laughed. The wind carried the sound away too soon for his liking.

"That's exactly why I don't run. No one looks happy while they're doing it. And it's hard on the knees. I walk. Besides, you see more of your surroundings that way, and the health benefits are just as good if you keep your pace brisk."

Kellen couldn't manage brisk at this point, but he was intrigued. "Where do you walk?"

"When it's too nasty to be outside, I use a treadmill."

"The one that's been moved to storage?"

"That would be the one." She wrinkled her nose. For the first time he noticed the freckles sprinkled across its slim bridge. "It's not a big deal. The weather has been nice lately. Besides, I like to walk on the beach. I'm a seashell addict."

He recalled the assortment of jars filled with shells spread around the house. Some people paid a decorator to bring in such touches. Brigit had collected them herself.

"Do they have a twelve-step program for that?"

She blinked. "Was that an actual joke you just made?"

"I used to have a good sense of humor."

"Did you break that in the accident, too?"

He laughed aloud, a rusty sound that scraped his throat as it came out, and sounded as foreign as it had that day he'd read the message she'd penned on the bathroom mirror.

"Funny. So, how often do you walk?"

"I try to carve out an hour every evening."

Every evening? Her toned legs and trim waist spoke of regular exercise. Still, he'd had no idea. He and Brigit were living under the same roof, but beyond sharing a cup of morning coffee on the deck, they had spent little time together. Part of the reason for that was her crazy work schedule. While he appreciated her dedication, since he benefited directly from it, once again he found himself wanting to know what drove her.

"Why do you do it?" he asked.

He was referring to the long hours she put in at the resort. Brigit, of course, assumed he was speaking about her evening walks.

"It's a good way to regroup mentally. And more obviously, it's a good way to work off calories so I can keep off the pounds."

She didn't look as if she had a problem with her weight. If anything she leaned toward too thin. He said as much.

"I used to be heavier."

Kellen worked hard to mask his surprise. He needn't have bothered. She wasn't looking at him. Her tone sounded far away when she added, "It was a long time ago. A lifetime ago. During an unhappy time in my life."

She closed her computer and rose to her feet just as Joe jogged up the steps that led from the sand. When the physical therapist reached the top, he stopped and bent at the waist, breathing heavily.

"Enjoy your run?" Brigit asked. She sent Kellen a wink.

"Y-yeah. Gr-great…morning…for it. The breeze…" He took one hand off his knees and motioned vaguely. "Kept me cool. It's…it's gonna be…a hot one."

"The humidity is expected to climb, too. The beach will be crowded. A lot of day-trippers come over from the mainland hoping to cool off on days such as this."

"Lou won't be fighting traffic at least," Joe remarked, having fully caught his breath, before he retreated inside.

Joe's comment brought back his worry about seeing the specialist in Charleston.

And his attorney.

Kellen rubbed his thigh. The daily regimen of ibuprofen he'd begun had dulled the worst of the pain, but nothing was successful in taking it away completely.

"Are you nervous?" Brigit asked.

He shook his head, but the words that came out of his mouth were, "A little. Okay, a lot."

He swung his legs over the side of the lounge chair, determined to stand. He didn't like being forced to look up at her, especially for a conversation in which he already had admitted vulnerability. He grabbed the railing and, using his upper body strength, levered to his feet. Brigit didn't offer any help. She merely waited until he was standing and steady on his feet to speak.

"I used to play this game with myself before… well, before I left my husband and took control of my life again. I'd ask myself, 'What's the worst thing that can happen?' Once I'd faced that fear, I knew I could handle anything."

The breeze kicked up, whipping several ribbons of dark hair across her face. This time, Kellen gave in to impulse and tucked it behind her ear before she could. It was as soft as silk, just as he'd suspected. Afterward, his hand lingered next to her cheek, his palm so close he could feel the heat from her skin.

He watched her eyes widen. In surprise? Interest? He needed to believe it was the latter. He needed to believe that he was still desirable. *Liar.* He needed to believe *she* found him desirable. He caressed her jaw before resting his palm against the curve of her cheek. Soft, so soft. Her lips parted ever so slightly, and Kellen leaned in and kissed her. When she didn't pull away, he went back for seconds.

He settled his mouth firmly over hers this time. Their noses bumped. She rose on tiptoe and tilted her head to one side. Problem solved. Now it was their bodies that brushed together. Or would have if the damned laptop she held hadn't been in the way. She remedied that issue, too. Without breaking off their kiss, she dropped the computer onto the lounge chair's cushions. Both of her hands were free now, and she brought them up to his shoulders.

Passion, the raw and unfettered kind, coursed through Kellen's veins. He welcomed it. Hell, he reveled in it. For the first time in months, he felt alive again. He felt…whole.

His left hand remained on the rail. He needed it there for support. But something told him that even if both of his legs had been working just fine, his knees would have felt weak. The kiss was that potent.

She pulled back slowly, blinking up at him as if in disbelief while she returned the heels of her feet to the deck's varnished boards. Although her hands remained on his shoulders, the moment was ending. Soon, all too soon, they would be back to the roles of business owner and employee. But Kellen didn't want this intriguing spell to be broken. Not yet.

He traced her bottom lip with the pad of his thumb and felt her shiver.

"Kellen. I don't think…" Her voice was barely a whisper. He leaned closer to hear her, but she shook her head. Whatever else she'd been about to say was snatched away by the wind.

"That game that you mentioned," he began. "What was your worst fear, Brigit?"

She didn't respond. Instead, she dropped her arms to her sides and backed up a step. Then, without another word, she turned and hurried inside, leaving him alone on the deck with far more questions left unanswered than the one he'd just asked.

CHAPTER SIX

"SORRY ABOUT THE change in plans," Brigit told her sister when they spoke on the phone later that same day.

"Don't worry about it." Brigit pictured her easy-going older sibling waving a hand in dismissal. They couldn't be more opposite. Brigit envied Robbie's roll-with-the-punches outlook. "We can come another time. As you wrote in your email, maybe we can plan a visit over Christmas break."

"Yes. Is Will upset?"

"He was looking forward to it," Robbie averred.

Brigit pictured her nephew's wide-set brown eyes, mop of reddish-brown hair and blunt chin. With every birthday he looked more like her late brother-in-law.

"I saw Scott in town."

This news had Brigit sitting up straighter in her office chair, a chill passing down her spine.

Even all these years later the mere mention of his name caused the old fears to coalesce. She swallowed, beat them back and let nonchalance take their place.

"What did he want?"

"He didn't *want* anything. In fact, we didn't speak. I just saw him while I standing in the supermarket checkout. He was a couple lanes down unloading groceries. He waved. I pretended I didn't see him."

"Did he…come any closer?"

"No. He's pretty careful to honor the restraining order."

Not only had Brigit taken out one against her insistent ex. So had her mother and her sister after he'd started showing up at their homes and places of work unannounced.

Brigit let out a silent sigh of relief. Nonetheless, she said, "I wish things could be different. I wish Scott could be different. I mean, he is Will's godfather." And with Mitch gone, he could have served as a much-needed father figure if he had been a better man.

"Don't remind me. But even if he had professed

to have changed, I wouldn't let that…that…*bully* near my son after the way he treated you. Some things are unforgivable." On this her easy-breezy sister's tone had turned implacable.

"I just hate making things harder for you and Mom in Arlis." Nearly everybody in the small southern Pennsylvania town thought Scott Wellington walked on water.

That was one of the reasons Brigit had changed her name back to Wright and decided to move after their divorce was finalized. Scott had made sure she'd been portrayed as the bad guy. She hadn't been able to prove it, but she was certain he'd been behind the rumors about an affair that had started just prior to their reaching a settlement. By that point she'd been happy to give him whatever he'd wanted just to get away.

Of course, he'd wanted Brigit. He'd wanted to continue to control her, to make her bend to his will and live her life according to his rules. She hadn't been about to let that happen. Not any longer.

So she'd signed over their house and all of its furnishings. She'd even let him keep the china that had been a wedding gift from her late grandmother. Whatever it had taken to get out from under his thumb, she'd done. She regretted giving him so much now. So many people in town had viewed her wholesale retreat as an affirmation of her guilt. Since her sister, nephew and mother still lived in Arlis, they were the ones who had to put up with the gossip mill. And five years later, it was still churning out tall tales.

"Mitch thought of Scott as a brother," Robbie said now. Indeed, Scott had served as best man at her wedding. "If he had known how controlling—"

But Mitch hadn't. No one had. After they'd wed, and Scott's rigid expectations had become intolerable, Brigit had kept quiet. She'd thought of her bad marriage as her own problem, her own private shame. And now she was determined that it all stay in the past.

Returning to the reason for her call, she told Robbie, "I hate having to disappoint Will."

"He'll be fine. And now he'll look forward to Christmas break all the more." Robbie cleared her throat and her tone turned sly when she asked, "So, what's Kellen Faust like in person? Do the photos I've seen of him shirtless on a beach in the Mediterranean do him justice?"

Almost all of the photos splashed over the internet and in the tabloids had been snapped pre-accident. His physique had been buff then, his skin tanned, toned and vital. Every inch of him had screamed fun-loving, hard-bodied stud. Now…

"He looks different," Brigit replied truthfully.

"Different good or different bad? Is it true that he can't walk?"

Even with her sister, Brigit didn't feel comfortable discussing the particulars of Kellen's condition. "You know how the entertainment media love to blow things out of proportion."

"So, he can walk?"

"He uses a cane, but, yes, he can walk."

"A cane, huh?"

"It makes him look sophisticated and…and sexy," she said in his defense, as if her sister were the sort of person who judged on appearances alone. "Sorry. It's just that he's very sensitive about it."

A long pause followed. So long a pause that Brigit thought the connection might have been lost. "Robbie? Are you still there?"

"Yep. Still here. So…sexy, huh?" Her sister made a humming noise. "That's an interesting description coming from you."

Brigit recalled the earlier kiss on the deck. It had awakened long-dormant desire, resurrected almost-forgotten needs. Rusty though she might have been when it came to intimacy, she recognized passion when she felt it, and she knew it had flowed both ways. Kellen had wanted her as badly as she'd wanted him. But the fact remained…

"He's my boss." She said it flatly. It served as a reminder to herself as well as an answer for her sister. "So, I think he's sexy. Big deal. I think the guy who plays Thor is sexy, too. It doesn't mean anything, Rob." She swallowed hard and forced herself to say it a second time. "It doesn't mean a thing."

Kellen wanted to break something. He wanted to hurl his damned cane across the examination room or punch a hole in the wall. He was even tempted to plow his fist into the doctor's face, as if it were the man's fault that Kellen's leg was shattered beyond repair.

He'd been foolish to come here. Foolish to hope for a better prognosis from this specialist when five of the guy's highly recommended peers already had told Kellen the same thing.

"You need to accept that your life has changed," the doctor was saying. "You can still live a full and active life, but it won't be the same active life you used to live. You need to find new hobbies, Mr. Faust. You need to figure out a new lifestyle. Other people in your position have. If you'd like, I can put you in touch with some of them."

"That's all right," he bit out.

The doctor cleared his throat. "I also recommend therapy."

"I'm in therapy," Kellen replied, pointing to Joe, who sat on a stool in the corner jotting down notes.

"I'm not talking about *physical* therapy, Mr. Faust," the doctor said. His expression was patient, kind…condescending. Kellen nearly did punch him in the face then.

To prevent that from happening, he balled his hands into fists in his lap as he sat on the exam table. He stayed that way for the remainder of the appointment.

"Sorry, Mr. F," Joe began as they left the doctor's office. "I know you were hoping for better news."

Kellen didn't answer. Once they were in the SUV, he barked an address at Lou. At least the attorney wouldn't be able to contradict Kellen's plans for his future.

More than ever, he needed to take over the helm at the resort. Be the one calling the shots. With so much else beyond his control, he needed to feel in charge of something. And the resort, the haven of his childhood, was all he had left.

After calling her sister, Brigit remained at the desk in her small office for most of the day on the pretext of catching up on paperwork. Hiding out was more like it. She was embarrassed, mortified, confused. What had come over her? She'd kissed her boss!

Technically, of course, Kellen had been the one to initiate contact. He'd tucked the hair back from her face, caressed her cheek and then… She hadn't seen it coming until that very moment. Still, he'd given her a chance to break it off and back away. Instead, what had she done? She'd put her arms around his shoulders, held on tight and kissed him right back. She'd even set down her laptop so she could do so. Set it down? She'd all but tossed it aside.

She pinched her eyes closed, dropped her head into her hands and groaned. The only thing more damning than that was the fact that she'd enjoyed it. Every blessed second and stroke of his tongue. It had been pure heaven.

Brigit wasn't sure she liked the man, even if she found him too attractive for her peace of mind. Over the past week, thanks in large part to those quiet mornings on the deck, they had developed a cordial relationship, one that still fell safely within the boundaries of being professional. She wouldn't pretend to understand him or what he'd been going through since his accident, but there seemed to be more to Kellen than the spoiled, apathetic heir she'd first assumed. She'd spied unexpected depths to go along with whatever demons it was that he fought.

But *cordial* didn't describe that kiss. Nothing about it had been friendly or casual. It had lit her up on the inside like a string of Christmas tree lights, and she swore they were still blinking maniacally, which just plain ticked her off.

She'd sworn off men after her divorce, eager to stand on her own two feet, determined to prove to herself that she'd never again let herself become spineless, worthless, invisible. She hadn't missed men, either.

Until now.

Damn Kellen! And damn her own foolishness!

Now what was she supposed to do? How was she supposed to act around him? Did she demand an apology? Or did she owe him one? What if he was expecting a repeat? She shivered even thinking of it, and loathed herself all the more when anticipation was the emotion that bubbled closest to the surface.

An hour later, she was still mentally berating herself when she heard two pairs of footsteps in the hall outside her office. One set was heavy, uneven and accompanied by the distinctive click of a cane on tile. The other was more measured. Kellen and Joe. They had returned from the mainland.

Act natural, casual, unaffected. Above all else, be professional. She exhaled through her mouth, rose to her feet. On her way to the door, she smoothed down her top and schooled her expression into one of polite interest.

"How did—?"

That was all she got out before Joe shook his head.

Kellen, meanwhile, never even glanced her way. He glared straight ahead with his jaw clenched, his sandy eyebrows pulled low over his eyes in a scowl reminiscent of the expression he'd been wearing during their first meeting.

Whatever news he'd received, it hadn't been good. Her heart sank. This, she knew, was Kellen's worst fear.

* * *

He took dinner in his room. Not just in the apartment, but in his bedroom. Brigit took the tray herself. Joe was at the apartment's kitchen peninsula, creating some kind of smoothie. He glanced up and smiled.

"Hey, Brigit. You're a gem. Just leave the tray on the counter. I'll take it in when I finish with this," he said as he added fresh banana slices to the blender.

That sounded good to her. The less interaction with Kellen the better. For both of them.

"Is that for Kellen?" She nodded to the blender.

"Are you kidding?" The physical therapist's laughter was subdued. "In his current mood Mr. F would probably chuck it at my head."

Brigit's anxiety over how to act around Kellen after their kiss was forgotten. She glanced down the hallway and lowered her voice to just above a whisper. "So, bad news today?"

"Not necessarily bad. Just not the news he wanted to hear." Joe stopped what he was doing, leaned his elbows on the counter and sighed. "This specialist basically told Mr. F the same thing all the other ones have. He won't be hotdogging down the slopes again. For that matter, he's never going to walk without a limp and a cane. The faster he comes to accept that and move on with his life, the better off he's going to be."

Joe straightened and resumed what it was he'd been doing. Soon the blender blades whirled, making conversation impossible.

Her heart ached. Poor Kellen. He must be devastated, she thought as she left the apartment.

Brigit stopped feeling sorry for him when, nearly a week later, he remained holed up in his bedroom with the curtains drawn. Joe had been the only visitor allowed to breach the threshold, and then only to bring Kellen his meals.

At first, she'd been almost relieved that Kellen hadn't joined her on the deck in the mornings. After that amazing kiss they'd shared, things between them were bound to be awkward and strained. But now, five days after his return from the doctor, she was out of both sympathy and patience.

The man had been dealt a bitter blow. No doubt

about that. But brooding wouldn't change anything. Brigit knew firsthand that self-pity got a person nowhere. He needed to concentrate on what was possible rather than on what wasn't.

Really, Kellen should be thanking his lucky stars. He could have suffered a massive head injury or broken his neck in the fall and become a quadriplegic. Despite his injuries, he was healthy overall. He had all of his mental faculties. He was still handsome, sexy, virile. Her body began to hum as she recalled their kiss. Oh, yeah. The accident had done nothing to diminish his sexual appeal. She swallowed, regrouped.

He was physically capable of working, even if he was wealthy enough that he didn't have to. Yes, he would have a limp and be required to use a cane for the rest of his life. But it wasn't the end of the world. He could trade in the ski slopes, his Swiss chalet and his sycophantic friends in Europe for a tropical island hideaway. There he could lie on a beach, surround himself with equally vacuous toadies and live comfortably off his inheritance, she thought uncharitably.

How many people could afford such a choice?

Brigit certainly hadn't been given many options when her life had crumbled into pieces before, and immediately after, her divorce. Putting those pieces back together had taken a Herculean effort. But she'd managed it. She was happy. Well, maybe not happy, but content.

Although lately… No. She shook off the thought that the solo, work-centric life she had planned might no longer be enough to satisfy her.

This wasn't about her. It was about Kellen and his future. And he could find contentment, too. First, however, he had to want it and put in the effort to attain it.

Joe was perched on the edge of the couch cushions watching a baseball game when she arrived with the evening's meal tray.

"You didn't have to bring Mr. F's dinner," the young man admonished as he rose to his feet. "I was heading to the dining room to eat after this inning and would have brought one back for him."

"That's all right. I was on my way here to change my clothes."

He consulted his watch. "It's a little early for

your evening walk. It hasn't even started to cool off outside yet."

Indeed, the mercury was still pushing ninety, which was why she usually waited until just before nightfall to comb the beach. With the exception of a handful of committed anglers, it was largely empty by then, even the most hard-core sunbathers having packed up for the day. Any shells that had washed ashore would be picked over, but she took a bag with her. Just in case. The beach always seemed to give up tiny treasures. Even after five years on Hadley Island, she wasn't able to resist collecting them.

"I know, but it's been a slow day. No new guests and the dinner crowd was light because of the music festival happening on the other side of the island." She set the tray on the kitchen counter and nodded toward the television. "So what's the score?"

Joe originally hailed from Florida, so he was grinning when he replied, "Tampa Bay is up by three runs in the top of the fourth."

"Go, Rays," she said without inflection. As expected, Joe laughed. Then she inclined her head toward the hallway. "Has he been out of his room at all today?"

"Nope. Never even got out of bed. He kept the shades pulled again, too." Joe shook his head. "It's like a tomb in there."

"That makes how many days now since his last physical therapy session?"

"Six. He's going to be extra sore once he finally decides to rejoin the land of the living."

She pursed her lips and shook her head.

"I know what you're thinking," Joe said.

"That he's so busy feeling sorry for himself he's sabotaging his recovery?" When Joe said nothing, Brigit tipped her head to the side. "Well, am I wrong?" she demanded.

"Not in the least."

This came from Kellen. He was in the hallway, standing just outside the door to the master bedroom. Despite the distance, he'd heard every word.

She swallowed and felt her face heat. "I'm sorry."

"Oh, please. Don't ruin your forthrightness with an apology," he told Brigit as he lumbered toward her. "Your honesty is one of the qualities I like best about you."

He was spoiling for a fight, and Brigit decided not to disappoint him. She notched up her chin. "All right. I'm not sorry. What I am is…disappointed."

Kellen's sandy brows lifted in surprise at that and he repeated, "Disappointed?"

Brigit settled her hands on her hips. "That's what I said. Disappointed."

Joe picked that moment to mumble something about going to dinner and wisely retreated. Kellen waited until the apartment door latched behind his physical therapist to continue.

"Yeah, well, get in line. I'm sure there's a spot open right behind my mother. I've never been able to do anything right in her opinion either." He shook his head. Some of the bluster went out of him. "She's right, of course. No one to blame for that but myself."

The comment momentarily threw Brigit. What the heck did his mother have to do with this? What was the woman right about? Another time, she might have asked him. But not right now.

Right now, she remained focused on the issue at hand: his reaction to this latest setback. She chose not to dwell on why it was so important to her that Kellen not give up.

Taking a step toward him, she demanded, "How can you expect to improve your condition if all you do is lie around and wallow in self-pity all day long?"

"Didn't Joe tell you? There's no improvement to be had. This is it, Brigit! What you see is what you get!"

Kellen's voice thundered through the apartment and he lifted his cane for emphasis. The mocking smile he sent her vanished when he lost his balance. He was able to catch himself on one of the island's stools before he crashed to the ground, but he had to let go of the cane to do so. The gold-tipped walking stick clattered to the floor, and a round of vicious cursing followed. Brigit allowed him to vent his frustration, waiting until he was done to continue speaking in a moderate tone.

"You're not going to be able to tackle the steep slopes in Europe again. You're not going to be able to run a marathon or a half marathon or even the island's annual two-block tyke trot. And it looks like competitive ballroom dancing will be a no-go, too."

"I don't need you to list all the things I can no longer do!" he shouted. Veins pulsed at his temples and his jaw clenched afterward.

She retrieved the cane and held it out to him. He snatched it away. If fire could have shot out from his eyes just then, Brigit figured her skin would have been charred. He was furious, but she took his rage in stride. After Scott, she'd vowed never to back down when she knew she was right. And she *was* right in this instance. She needed to make Kellen use his rage to his advantage. Channeled correctly, it could be beneficial. God knew, she'd used her own anger as a catalyst for change. She was proud of all she had accomplished since then, proud of the way she'd taken the bull by the proverbial horns and reinvented herself rather than succumbing to despair.

So she ignored his temper and went on. "All right. I'll tell you what you *can* do. Based on your current physical condition and attitude, you can continue to be an embittered invalid."

She expected her words to get a rise out of him. To her consternation, the fight went out of Kellen. His voice lost its steely edge and he stated flatly, "I *am* an invalid, Brigit, bitter or otherwise."

"Joe thinks you could get stronger if you followed his advice to the letter rather than skipping days at a time and then putting in minimal effort when you finally do show up."

"So you and Joe are discussing my therapy? I wasn't aware I was a topic of conversation between the two of you."

He was trying to make her feel bad, but she wouldn't let him. "You know what your problem is, Kellen?"

He blew out a breath. "I'm sure you're only too happy to tell me."

"As a matter of fact..." She smiled sweetly and went on. "Your problem, Kellen, is that you're expecting someone to wave a magic wand and hand you back your good health."

"Bull—"

"I'm not finished," she interrupted.

And Brigit sincerely hoped that she wasn't, career-wise especially. Her bluntness could wind up costing her big-time, but the fact remained that the man needed a swift kick in the seat of his designer-label track pants. Since no one else seemed inclined to do it, she would do the honors. The faster he was back on his feet—literally as well as figuratively—the faster he would leave and things could get back to normal at the resort.

Brigit ignored the twinge of regret the thought of his leaving caused. She ignored the small voice that whispered she would miss him. Instead, she plowed ahead, intentionally discarding any effort to employ tact. Politeness would only get in the way at this point. Kellen needed to hear the unvarnished truth.

"You have the power to change your circumstances. You may not be able to return to what you used to be. But being happy, carving out a fulfilling future, those things are up to you."

"Is that what you did, Brigit?"

The question caught her off guard. "What do you mean?"

"After your divorce. You tucked yourself away on Hadley Island, threw yourself into your work.

"You don't know anything about my marriage or my divorce."

"Easily remedied," he murmured, eyebrows lifted. Even if she had been tempted, the offer to spill her secrets was hardly sincere.

"We aren't talking about me."

"Handy." He cocked his head to one side. "Are you happy, Brigit? Are you *fulfilled*?"

The way he said it, the way he looked at her had needs she'd nearly forgotten bubbling to the surface. She chose to ignore both his question and her dormant desires and took a breath. "We're talking about you. Ask yourself, Kellen, is this how you want to spend the rest of your life? Being angry and unpleasant and acting defeated? If it is, then I hope you will find somewhere else to do it."

His mouth fell open for a moment before he asked in disbelief, "Are you telling me to leave my own resort?"

"No."

"Really? Because that's sure as hell what it sounded like to me, Brigit."

"What I'm saying is that no one wants to be around someone who is irritable and angry all of the time."

"Yourself included? You don't want to be around me? You didn't seem all that adverse the other day on the deck." His tone was suggestive; his gaze slid down her body slowly before returning to her mouth.

"Don't."

"Don't what?" he challenged, his tone retaining all of its redolence.

"Don't be a jerk. Don't treat me like one of the brainless ski bunnies who hang out at your chalet."

"Because you're better than that?" he asked snidely.

She blinked, regrouped. After only a moment's hesitation she replied. "You're damned right I am. But actually, what I was thinking is that *you're* better than that."

She'd hoped to snap him out of his funk, but her words only seemed to make him angrier.

"This is me, Brigit. Don't like it, then get the hell out. I can replace you in a heartbeat."

Something inside of her went cold. For one panicky second, old insecurities threatened to overwhelm her. They battered her self-esteem the way waves battered the coast during a Category 5 hurricane.

You're so helpless, Brigit.

You're so incompetent.

How stupid can a person be?

You should be thanking your lucky stars every day that someone like me wanted to marry someone as naive and backward as you.

She mentally swatted away Scott's belittling remarks, angry with herself for letting them back in for even a moment. At least with Kellen, she understood why he was lashing out. Scott had sought to hurt and demean her for the pure sport of it. That kind of cruelty was incomprehensible to her.

Kellen was saying, "Faust Haven is mine. My grandfather left it to me. So I'll stay here as long as I damned well please. That is my right!"

The heir had spoken. A couple of weeks ago,

she might have believed his imperious act. But she'd glimpsed the man behind the curtain, knew him to be vulnerable, lost.

"That is your right," she agreed calmly, even though her pulse was still pinging on high. "And I'm sure finding another manager would be easy. You found a few before me."

She loved her job. She loved the island. She would be devastated to be forced to leave and start over. Where would she go? How would she land another position with a black mark such as being fired for insubordination on her résumé? And how could she leave Kellen?

The last question caught her by surprise. Nothing was going on between them. A kiss and some friendly banter did not make a relationship. And then there was the fact that he was her boss.

"But?" he pressed as she puzzled over her feelings.

Briefly, she wondered if she should cut her losses and apologize. In his current mood, he might very well fire her. Brigit swallowed and backed up a step, but she didn't retreat. She couldn't. She wasn't done having her say and, if her joke of a marriage to Scott had taught her nothing else, it had taught her to hold her ground, because never again would she allow herself to be turned into a self-effacing coward afraid to voice her opinion.

"But they won't be as good as I am." She swallowed and added, "At my job."

"Is that all?"

Her palms were damp. She ignored the telltale moisture as she gripped them together. "No. That's not all. The point I am trying to make, Kellen, is that whether you stay on Hadley Island or go back to Europe or—" she motioned with one hand "—park your rear end at the North Pole, no one wants to be around a person who is determined to wallow in his misery."

"Do you think I enjoy being miserable?" he asked, sounding incredulous.

"No, but you've accepted it. Heck, you've embraced it."

There was no backing down now. She'd opened this particular can of worms and she would see it through. But, God, she hoped the walls were thick enough to prevent the resort's guests from overhearing their heated exchange.

"I've done the damned exercises. They don't help. Nothing helps!"

"Please," she spat with a shake of her head. "You only get out of physical therapy what you are willing to put into it. Can you honestly say that you've done the exercises faithfully?" When he glanced away, she knew she had him and so she pressed on. "You have the money to hire a personal physical therapist. He's at your disposal 24/7. He lives under the same roof as you do, for heaven's sake. Do you have any idea how many other people recovering from serious accidents would love to be in your position?"

"I know I'm fortunate, but you make it sound so easy."

She moderated her tone and dropped the volume. "That's not my intent. I know it's hard and painful and the odds may be stacked against you. But at least you have options, Kellen. And you have a lot to be grateful for." She place a hand on his arm. "You walked away from an accident that could have left you confined to a wheelchair for the rest of your life. If you can't work up a little gratitude for that alone, then maybe you injured your head in the fall, too."

He closed his eyes momentarily, and she thought she might have gotten through to him, but then he demanded, "Are you done?"

"I…I guess I am," she replied, exasperated with both of them. Why did it matter to her what he did? She wasn't his keeper.

"Good." He pointed to the tray of food that sat forgotten on the countertop. "I'd like to eat on the deck tonight."

He turned and started for the door. Apparently, he expected her to carry the tray outside for him. He was back to his heir act. And she his dutiful underling. She picked it up. The cheery yellow daisy in the bud vase mocked her. She might be his employee, but she damned well wouldn't be his enabler. Even if it cost Brigit her job, she'd be damned if she would allow herself to be marginalized. Not again. *Never* again. She returned the tray to the countertop with enough force to cause the dishes to rattle and the iced tea to slosh over the rim of its glass.

"You carry it," she told him.

He glared back at her. "What?"

"You heard me."

He snorted. "Very funny. I can't and you know it."

"That's right. So, you know that that means?" She didn't wait for him to respond, but held up a finger. "A, you need to be nicer to the people who are helping you, whether they are paid or not." Holding up a second finger, she added, "And B, you need put more effort in to improve your situation."

"Do you think this is what I want?" His voice had turned soft, but she wasn't fooled by the muted tone. He was every bit as angry as he had been moments ago. Maybe even more so based on the way his face now flushed scarlet. That anger wasn't directed at her, at least not intentionally, and once again she found herself thinking how, channeled correctly, his intense emotions could prove a benefit rather than a hindrance to his recovery.

"I think—"

That was as far as she got before he cut her off.

"Do you think this is how I want to live? Having people help me stand and sit and carry my plate? I hate this! I. Hate. This!" He brought the cane down on the edge of the granite countertop with such force that it snapped in two. One half flew into the living room. The other flipped end over end before striking Brigit just under her chin. The jagged wood pierced her flesh. Pain mingled with surprise as she clapped her hand over the wound. Her fingers came away bright red.

The color drained from Kellen's face.

"My God! Brigit, I never meant…"

He reached for her, but she batted his fingers away with her bloody hand.

More frustrated than anything, she turned and rushed out of the apartment, passing a wide-eyed Joe as she sought the refuge of her office.

CHAPTER SEVEN

KELLEN WAS DISGUSTED with himself. What kind of a monster had he become? Of course he hadn't intended for the cane to snap and strike Brigit, but the fact remained—that was exactly what had occurred. His rage had caused her injury. And all she'd been trying to do was help him.

He rubbed a hand over his face as he slid down the wall to the floor. Never had he hated himself more. Brigit was right. He had a lot to be grateful for. Self-pity would get him nowhere. Hell, his mother was right. He needed to grow up, take responsibility for his life, be the man his grandfather had believed Kellen could be.

He'd thought he'd been doing that by coming to the island, determined to learn the ropes and eventually take over the day-to-day management of the inn. But he'd been fooling himself. He'd come here to hide not to heal. He'd been so stuck in the past that living the present, much less having dreams for the future, had been impossible.

He was still seated on the floor when Joe rushed in several minutes later.

"Mr. F?" The young man's eyes were rounded with concern. "Brigit's in her office and… Wh-what happened? Are you all right?"

Kellen wasn't sure how to respond. He wasn't all right, but it had nothing to do with his leg. So, instead of replying, he asked, "Can you help me up? Please."

"Sure thing."

With Joe's assistance, Kellen was soon on his feet with his back braced against the wall.

"What happened to your cane?" Joe retrieved one of the pieces from the floor.

Kellen's gut clenched on a potent mixture of embarrassment and shame. "If you don't mind, I'd rather not talk about it right now."

"Okay. Sure. No problem." The therapist bobbed his head in affirmation.

That was Joe, eager to please, unable to call his boss on the carpet for either his actions or his attitude. Unlike Brigit, who'd given Kellen a piece of her mind even though it meant having to step into the line of fire. Literally. Kellen pictured her bloodied chin again and a fresh wave of shame swamped him. He wasn't fit company.

"I'd like to return to my room. I want to..." To what? *Hide* was the word that taunted him, but he said, "I want to go lie down."

"Right now, Mr. F?" Joe frowned. "But you only just got up."

"I know, Joe. My room," he repeated. "Therapy tomorrow, I promise, but right now I have a lot to think about."

The therapist pointed to the tray. "I can have your dinner warmed up, if you want. The chicken was excellent tonight, and a good source of protein."

Kellen shook his head.

Given the way his stomach was churning, he doubted he would be able to keep down anything.

The following morning, Kellen made his way out to the deck even before the sun was fully up. Without his cane, he'd had to call on Joe for assistance. He'd hoped to see Brigit sitting in her usual spot, drinking coffee, the computer open on her lap. God knew, he needed to apologize, to beg her for forgiveness if need be. He'd acted abominably. But the deck was empty.

"Looks like I beat Brigit out here today," he said in what he hoped sounded like a conversational tone rather than that of a man desperate to make amends.

Joe helped him into one of the lounge chairs, waiting until he was settled to say, "I'd imagine she's going to sleep late today."

"Oh? Why do you say that?" Kellen asked.

"She didn't get back from the emergency room on the mainland until after three this morning."

"Emergency room?" And Kellen had thought he couldn't feel any worse than he already did.

"I called Lou and asked him to take her. She didn't want to go, but that gash on her chin was pretty bad."

Swallowing hard, Kellen asked, "How bad?"

"Bad enough that it needed to be closed with stitches." Joe studied Kellen without blinking. Questions brewed in the other man's eyes, but all he said was, "It's too bad about her slipping on the floor and hitting her chin on the island."

"Is that what she said happened?"

"Yep." Joe nodded. "That's what she said, all right."

For the first time since Kellen had known Joe, the man's affable smile and easygoing nature were nowhere to be found. He couldn't blame the guy for being suspicious, and while Kellen didn't owe his employee any explanations, he felt the need to clear the air and own up to his responsibilities.

"It was my fault," he said.

Joe's gaze turned as cold as a tombstone. In the instant before Kellen went on, he knew that the seemingly friendly giant of a man was fully capable of violence should the situation call for it. Even though that violence would have been directed at Kellen, he found a new respect for the guy.

"I struck the counter with my cane. It broke and the halves went flying. One of them struck Brigit on the chin." He swallowed hard, but the sour taste remained in his mouth.

"So it was an accident," Joe said, some of the tension ebbing from his broad shoulders.

Kellen nodded. "But it was still entirely my fault and I feel sick about it. She was only trying to be helpful."

But it was time he helped himself.

That was the realization he'd come to last night, as he'd sat alone in his room replaying not only his conversation with Brigit, but reviewing how he'd spent the four months since his accident. Hell, how he'd spent his adulthood. He been dealt some hard knocks, but that was no excuse for his behavior.

It had taken a blunt-spoken employee to finally make him see the light. He pictured Brigit, and amended, a pretty, blunt-spoken woman with dark-lashed blue eyes who saw through his bluster to the man beneath.

Suddenly, it was vitally important that she like what she saw.

Brigit changed the bandage on her chin in the small restroom off her office. In the three days since her visit to the ER, the flesh surrounding the gash had turned from deep purple to mottled red to an unsightly bluish-green. She had a feeling it would turn a couple more unattractive colors yet before finally fading. As for the wound itself, it was going to scar. No way around that, as the ER doctor had confirmed. But it was low enough on her chin that it wouldn't be very visible. No one was likely to see it unless they stooped down in front of her and then looked up.

Well, it was her own damned fault. She'd pushed Kellen too far. He'd passed his breaking point as surely as his cane had when it had met the granite countertop's edge. For the past few days she'd tried unsuccessfully to get his guilt-stricken expression out of her head. Indeed, she'd done her best not only to avoid thinking about it, but to avoid him. That meant coming into the apartment late at night and leaving before it was light the following day. She missed her early mornings on the deck, watching the sun scatter muted gold rays across the horizon. She missed Kellen and his quiet presence. But she took her coffee at her desk and kept the door closed while she was in there. Not surprisingly, she was able to find plenty to do to keep her busy.

Are you happy, Brigit? Are you fulfilled?

She did her best to forget his questions. They were irrelevant, she assured herself.

As for Kellen, it was none of her business if he wanted to forgo his physical therapy and sit around feeling sorry for himself. None at all, even if she could admit she was attracted to him. Why then, she wondered, did she still feel the need to do something to help him?

She blamed the kiss, even as she sought to discount it. So, they'd locked lips in one of the most amazing kisses of her life. Big deal. That didn't make her his keeper. It didn't make her *anything* to Kellen. They were adults. Two lonely people looking for…nothing.

Brigit wasn't looking for anything. She had a job she loved, one that she wanted to continue doing well into the future. To ensure that she got that chance, she needed to stay out of his personal business. Sooner or later, despite his familial attachment to Faust Haven, he would get bored and leave. Then her life would get back to normal. And their relationship would return to one marked by intermittent professional correspondence via the internet. She ignored the hollowed out feeling in her gut. That was what she wanted. Okay, maybe not what she wanted, but it was all she could expect.

That evening while she finished logging in a couple of Sherry's last-minute changes to the week's dinner menu an email dropped into her inbox.

She knew the sender well. *FunLuver17,* a moniker that could be taken a couple of ways. Ambivalent, just like the man.

The subject line read: Need your assistance, please

Please? Hmm, the bow to manners was a new twist. As was his admitting to needing some help. Curiosity got the better of her and she clicked on the email.

Dear Miss Wright, it began.

So, they were back to courtesy titles. She should have been pleased. In the absence of physical distance, emotional distance would be for the best. But disappointed was what Brigi felt. Irritated with herself, she shrugged it off and continued reading.

Joe has the night off.

She knew that, of course. Lou had come to collect him. The two men were heading to Little John's Crab Shack a couple miles up the beach for a late dinner and some live entertainment. Joe had stopped by the office on his way out to tell her that Kellen was in bed—whether again or still, she hadn't asked—and not likely to need anything. Well, apparently, Joe had been wrong.

Could you bring a dinner tray?

Many thanks, KF

She closed the email and sighed. He had used *please* and *thanks*. So much for her efforts to avoid him.

The apartment was quiet when she entered holding the tray. Quiet and dark. The shades were drawn even though sunlight stole in around the edges. No wonder Joe had been eager for a night out. It was depressing in here.

"Hello?" she called.

As tempted as she was just to leave the tray on the kitchen counter and leave, she had to be sure Kellen could get to it. He still didn't have a cane, but Joe had mentioned finding a piece of driftwood on the beach during one of his morning runs. He'd trimmed off a couple knobby outcroppings and had cut it down to the proper size. According to Joe, it would do until the new one Kellen had ordered arrived.

"In here."

His bedroom. Of course.

The last thing she wanted to do was confront the lion in his den, but she swallowed, notched up her bandaged chin and breezed in holding the tray aloft.

A lamp burned at his bedside. The base was clear glass, which she'd filled with shells. She nudged a book out of the way so that she could set the tray on the nightstand.

Kellen sat on the bed with his back against the upholstered headboard. His good leg was bent at the knee, foot planted squarely on the mattress. He wore his usual nylon track pants and cotton T-shirt, this one with a quarter-size designer logo embroidered on the breast.

That was as far as she allowed her gaze to stray. She didn't make eye contact.

"Here you go," she told him in lieu of a greeting. "I think you'll enjoy it. Sherry's stuffed pork tenderloin always gets rave reviews from our guests. The portion size is smaller than what we serve in the dining room, but Joe insisted on no more than a playing card–size portion and double the amount of veggies."

With that she turned to leave. She made it almost to the door before Kellen said, "I think I will eat on the deck tonight."

Her back was still to him, so she could grimace and mutter a curse under her breath without him seeing. Then she turned, a forced smile curving her mouth while she returned for the tray.

As tempting as she found it to dump the sliced pork, red-skinned potatoes and steamed asparagus tips over his head, she resisted. The chef had worked too hard on the meal to treat it with such disrespect, and besides, Brigit would be the one who would have to clean it up.

"Certainly, Mr. Faust," she said in her most dutiful tone.

"I prefer you call me Kellen," he told her as he maneuvered to the edge of the bed.

"I thought since your email referred to me as Miss Wright…" She let her words trail off and shrugged.

"I did that out of respect," he told her quietly as he struggled to stand.

Out of respect? Hmm. What to make of that?

Even though she was confused, she replied, "I see."

For the first time since entering the room, she glanced at his face. He looked like hell. The dark smudges under his eyes made it look as if he'd gone a few rounds in the ring with a prize-fighter, and from the prickly growth on his jaw it was clear he hadn't shaved in days. His hair was unkempt, tufts going this way and that on his crown. Despite all the time he'd spent in bed, he hardly appeared rested.

"May I…may I call you Brigit?" he asked quietly. His gaze was on her bandaged chin, and an emotion she'd never seen before glazed his eyes.

Where he had been irritable and bitter at their last meeting, this time he appeared subdued, humbled. Rather than making demands and hurling out edicts, he was asking for permission to call her by her given name.

Her heart warmed, melted in a way that spelled danger. Still, how could she say no?

"I…I…" She recalled their kiss, the passion it had ignited. Under the circumstances it seemed ridiculous not to be on a first-name basis. "That's fine."

He nodded and reached for the walking stick tucked next to the nightstand. Sand and water had worn off the bark, leaving the grayish-brown wood smooth. The top curved just enough to make the perfect handle.

"Joe told me about the piece of driftwood he found."

"It does the job," Kellen agreed.

She collected the tray. Before she could turn to go, he said quietly, "Brigit?"

"Yes?"

"How…how is your chin?"

"It's fine."

"Joe said you had to go to the emergency room for stitches."

"Actually, they used glue. The wonders of modern medicine. No needles and no stitches to be removed later. I just need to keep the area clean and dry." She forced a laugh.

His expression remained sober. "Did they say if it would scar?"

"Probably." She shrugged.

"God!" He bit off an oath, and reassured her, "I'll pay for you to see a plastic surgeon. The best money can buy."

"That won't be necessary. I'm not a vain woman, and even if I was, it's not in an obvious place."

She watched his throat work. When he spoke, his voice was hoarse. "I'm sorry, Brigit. You have to believe me. I never meant for—"

"It was an accident, Kellen."

"Still, it was my fault that you got hurt."

Angry and bitter, Kellen had been easier to resist. But standing in front of her looking tortured and acting humbled and contrite? Her heart kicked out a couple extra beats and that was before his eyes locked with hers. Under his current scrutiny she felt more self-conscious than she had when his gaze had first homed in on her chin.

"Apology accepted," she mumbled.

Then, tray in hand, Brigit hurried from the room.

She took his dinner outside, bypassing the lounge chairs and setting the tray on the wrought-iron bistro table tucked into the corner of the deck. By the time she returned inside, he had reached the French doors. She held one open for him. Their bodies brushed innocently as he stepped outside. He stopped and held her gaze. The fingers of his free hand grazed her cheek. She remembered that light touch. Helpless to do otherwise, she pressed her cheek against his outstretched palm.

"I want…I would like…" He pinched his eyes closed and exhaled slowly. Then, "Will you stay? With me? Please."

"I just assumed you would want to be alone."

He took a seat on one of the heavy wrought iron chairs she'd pulled out for him. Rueful laughter followed. "I don't know what I want anymore. Well, except that I'd like you to keep me company. If you have the time. Please."

Her breath hitched as he stared up at her. This was not the entitled heir who had arrived at the resort mere weeks earlier. Nor was it the bitter man who'd neglected his therapy sessions despite desperately wanting to get better. And it certainly wasn't the angry and frustrated man who'd vented his ire just the night before. The man before her was contrite. Open in a way she'd never seen him before.

She swallowed. This was the kind of man who could make her believe in the happily ever after Scott's abusive ways had destroyed.

Her head told her to politely decline Kellen's invitation, but it was her battered heart she heeded as she slid on to the chair opposite his and adjusted the angle so that she could look out at the ocean. While he ate, she took in the scenery beyond the waving grass that topped the sand dune. She'd always loved this view and the privacy of the deck, which was bounded on either side by vine-covered trellises whose blooms scented the sea air.

It was a hot evening, the humidity almost oppressive. People who were not used to it often complained and preferred the air-conditioning of the dining hall to eating alfresco. In truth, she was surprised that Kellen had wanted to come outdoors, but after holing up in his room for a few days, maybe he'd felt the need for a change of scenery regardless of the heat that accompanied it.

"Hot night," he said, almost as if he could read her mind.

"Humid, too," she replied just to make conversation. What topic could be safer than the weather? So she went on. "I heard on the news tonight that temperatures are expected to hover in the nineties until the weekend."

"Beach will be crowded."

She made a humming noise that passed for agreement.

Kellen set his fork aside with a clatter. "You must think I'm the biggest jerk in the world."

Brigit blinked, caught off guard by his blunt statement. "Actually, I reserve that title for my ex. Besides, it's not my place to make judgments."

"Because I'm your boss."

She could have agreed and left it at that. Perhaps she should have. But it wasn't the truth and even though she couldn't figure out why, she felt that she owed him that much.

"I did things I wasn't proud of when I…when I was going through a rough patch in my life."

"Your divorce, you mean?"

It wasn't something she talked about often. Even with her sister and mother, Brigit had been stingy with the details. She'd found them too painful to recount, too humiliating to admit to. But she nodded.

"When it came right down to it, I had a choice to make. I could stay and accept my life as it had become, which was pretty bad, or I could leave. It sounds simple—" she sent him a wry smile "—unless you're the one taking the big leap and not at all sure where you're going to land." She reached across the table and laid her hand over his. She meant it to be friendly, but she also wanted to touch him. To connect. "Change is never easy, Kellen."

He grunted. "I admire you, Brigit."

"Me?" She blinked in surprise.

"Yes, you. And I respect you. I may sign your paycheck, but you're not afraid to speak your mind, even if it's to tell me that I'm being an ass."

"I don't remember using that exact word," she mumbled.

"The sentiment was the same." Humor lurked in his tone, but then he went on. "It may not seem like it, especially after the way I acted the other night, but I do value your opinion, and not just on matters that pertain to the resort. I guess what I'm trying to say is…" He looked away and she watched his Adam's apple bob. "I need you, Brigit."

A lump formed in her own throat. She'd never been needed before, not by a man. Especially not by a man she'd criticized, even if that criticism was warranted and intended to be constructive. She didn't know what to say.

"Speechless, I see," he said after a long silence.

"More like flattered."

He shifted in his chair, grimaced.

"What did the doctor say about pain?" Brigit asked.

"It's to be expected, but should lessen over time." Kellen picked up his knife and fork and cut off another bite of pork. "Sometimes I think I should have let them amputate my damned leg. At least I'd be in less pain," he muttered before popping the meat into his mouth.

"That's defeat talking."

Kellen bobbed his head. "But I'm not giving up."

"Good."

"You'll appreciate this. He offered to give me something in the interim."

"And you turned him down," she guessed.

"Actually, I asked him for a non-narcotic alternative. He prescribed a high-potency ibuprofen." His wry laughter floated away on the breeze. After a few minutes of silence, Kellen asked, "So, do you think this doctor could be wrong?"

"Wrong is a strong word," Brigit said slowly. The last thing she wanted was to give Kellen false hope. But… "You might be able to improve the prognosis."

"If I put in more effort, you mean."

She nodded. "I'm not saying you'll ever be one hundred percent, Kellen. That's not going to happen and you need to accept that. But accepting isn't the same as admitting defeat. There's no reason to embrace your current condition."

She expected an argument, but he nodded.

He picked up his glass and took a sip. His grimace was comical. "I've been meaning to tell you, this stuff is awful."

"It's tea. Iced tea," she added unnecessarily, given the cubes that tinkled against the sides of the glass.

"But it's not sweet. This is the South, Brigit. We take our iced tea with lots of sugar down here."

She wondered if he was aware that as he spoke his tone took on a noticeable drawl.

"Yes, well, not all of the guests who stay at Faust Haven are from the South. In fact, a good number of them hail from points north, especially in the winter. We keep packets of sugar on the tables in the dining room so guests can sweeten their own drinks. I must have forgotten to put some on the tray for you. If you'd like, I can go get you some."

She was already rising when he said, "I'd rather have wine. How about if you bring a bottle of red?" When she hesitated, he added, "I'm not driving."

Nor, as he'd just explained, was he taking any medications that would restrict alcohol consumption.

"All right."

As she started for the door, he stopped her with a new request. "And bring two glasses." The corners of his mouth lifted. "One for you."

"Oh, no wine for me. I'm on the clock." She winked. "What would my boss say?"

"He'd say, you're no longer on the clock. I'm giving you the night off. Have Danny cover for you."

"He's nineteen and the bellboy!" she exclaimed. "Besides, he's already gone home for the night."

"Someone else then."

"Kellen—"

His gaze had been on the horizon, where the waves were capped briefly in white before they churned to shore. Now his eyes shifted to her.

"Have a drink with me, Brigit? Please."

She'd been attracted to the man who'd issued commands and barked orders. To the one who now asked politely and extended invitations, she was putty. That should have made her nervous. But she suspected the butterflies flitting about in her stomach had a far different origin. "One bottle of red and two glasses coming up."

CHAPTER EIGHT

BRIGIT RETURNED FIFTEEN minutes later.

Holding the neck of an opened bottle of merlot in one hand and the stems of a pair of wine goblets in the other. Her movements were deft, economical and sexy despite that.

A sigh whispered out before he could prevent it, and the smile he sent her was genuine. He'd meant what he'd said about needing her. But at that moment, it wasn't Brigit's frankness he was admiring.

"Louise is at the reception desk, in case you were wondering," she said.

Kellen mentally shifted gears. "Louise?" he asked, trying to picture the employee in question. He'd met most of the staff over the past few weeks, but only in passing. That would have to change, of course. He needed to know who was responsible for what.

Birgit was saying, "She works in housekeeping, but I've been training her to work the desk. She's young, but capable. And she knows where to find me if anything comes up that she can't handle on her own." Merlot poured, she set the bottle aside and slipped into her seat. "Thank you, by the way."

"For?"

"The wine. Although, now that I think about it, I should have picked one of the pricier labels. We stock a couple vintages that I can't afford on my salary."

"Maybe you're due a raise then."

"Maybe I am." She sent him a sideways smile as she lifted her glass and tapped it against his.

After the quasi toast, they both took a sip.

"This is good," he said, turning the bottle so he could read the label. His brows shot up in surprise. "Medallion Winery?"

"It's a vineyard in Northern Michigan," she said.

"Yes, I've heard of it. I met the owner, Zack Holland, a couple of years ago when I accepted a friend's invitation to ski the slopes in Aspen for a couple weeks. He was on vacation with his new wife, Jane. No, Jaye. Very outspoken woman." He smiled. "You remind me of her."

"I'll take that as a compliment," Brigit said.

"Good, because I intended it as one." Kellen studied the contents of his glass. "They talked up their wine and some of the awards it had won, but I wasn't expecting…"

"They had an excellent year in 2007. In fact, this vintage earned a couple of prestigious awards, which is why Sherry asked me to order a few cases to serve at the inn. According to her, it pairs well with her stuffed pork tenderloin."

Kellen spared a glance at his forgotten meal and nodded thoughtfully before agreeing, "It does."

They both took another sip.

"Are you a connoisseur?" he asked.

"I wouldn't say that." She wrinkled her nose and laughed. He liked the sound. "I just do a little research, even if I also rely on the experts when ordering for the inn. You probably know more about wine than I do."

"Not really. I just know what I like." He realized his gaze was on the woman rather than his wine, so he held up his glass and studied the deep red liquid in the waning light. "Dry and medium-bodied. I've never been able to pick up the aromas of this and notes of that the experts talk about."

"Same here."

She chuckled again and settled back in her chair, almost as if she were becoming relaxed. Kellen knew he was. His shoulder muscles, which were always so tense, had started to loosen. And while his leg still ached, the throbbing had subsided, so much so that he was able to ignore it.

Which reminded him. "Don't tell Joe."

"About the wine?"

"He doesn't want me drinking during my recovery."

"But you aren't taking any medications that require abstinence," she replied. "A glass of wine shouldn't hurt."

"I know, but he has this very holistic approach to my rehabilitation, including diet and nutrition."

"His smoothies?"

"For starters."

"And you've followed his advice religiously," she replied drolly.

"He can be a tyrant."

"Joe?"

He nodded. "At first, he tried to ban all caffeine unless it came in the form of green tea. I can't live without my morning coffee."

"Yes, and I'm sure you were very diplomatic when you explained that to him."

Kellen had bellowed his protest in blistering fashion. Brigit's wry expression told him she'd guessed as much.

"I made him see reason."

She sipped her wine. "Green tea is very good for you. Antioxidants and such."

"Do you drink it?"

"I've tried it," she said slowly.

"Then you know that it tastes like steeped grass clippings."

"Having never tasted steeped grass clippings, I will defer to your judgment."

"Come on. Just admit that you don't like it," he coaxed.

Her eyes held as much amusement as challenge when she replied, "It's not my favorite beverage, but then I don't care for black tea either. Satisfied?"

Satisfied? At the moment, Kellen was far from it. But he grunted out an affirmation anyway, since the source of his dissatisfaction was difficult to determine. All he knew was that suddenly worries about his busted-up leg and concerns for his future—the two things that had dominated his life—had been replaced by other thoughts.

He and Brigit didn't speak for the next several minutes. The sound of the waves and the chatter and squawk of seabirds hunting for their evening meal occasionally broke the silence. As did snippets of conversation from beachcombers or guests on the inn's public decks.

"I love this place." He didn't realize he'd spoken the words aloud until she glanced over, her expression making it clear that she was waiting for him to go on. He usually didn't talk about his childhood, not even the good parts. But he did now. "I came here almost every summer when I was a boy."

"Sounds like heaven," she murmured. "I spent my summers at YMCA day camps until I was old enough to take care of myself. My mom worked."

"And your father?"

"Gone."

"I'm sorry. My father died when I was a kid, too. Cancer." His grandfather had tried to shield Kellen from as much of the disease's cruelty as possible, but the image of his father's gaunt frame and sunken eyes remained burned into Kellen's memory to this day. It was just another reason he considered the resort such a sanctuary. He had good memories here. Happy ones. The kind every kid, rich or poor, should have.

Brigit snapped him out of his reverie by saying, "My dad didn't die. Shortly after I was born, he simply opted out of fatherhood. He wasn't part of either my life or my older sister's."

There was no *simple* about it, regardless of her matter-of-fact tone. Kellen asked, "But he supported you, right?"

"Financially, you mean?" At his nod, she shook her head. "My mother said he wasn't the sort who could hold a job for long."

Kellen tried to digest that. Money had never been an issue in his household, or so he'd thought at the time. After his father's death, his mother had been faced with a lot of bills and not a lot left in her savings once she'd paid them. The experience had left her angry with her late husband and estranged from the son who reminded her so much of him.

For better or worse, he and Brigit each had been shaped by their upbringings. The nuggets of information he had mined from Brigit over the past few weeks offered an interesting glimpse into what had created her self-sufficient and direct personality. She didn't need men. The ones who had been in her life—father and husband—had disappointed her. Or worse? He wondered.

"Sorry," Kellen offered a second time.

She shook her head. "I'm not. It's hard to miss something you never had. Besides, my mom more than made up for his absence. She is smart, capable, determined and very independent."

And the apple hadn't fallen far from the tree, he thought. "Then I'd say you're lucky."

"What's your mom like?"

The question was innocuous and in keeping with the conversation. Still, it caught him off guard. He offered the first description that came to mind. "Hard."

"Hard?"

"Hard to please. Hard to live with. Hard to love. We don't have much of a relationship. Haven't since my dad died when I was eleven. I'm just like him, apparently." Even as he said it, Kellen held on to his grandfather's explanation that it wasn't actual resentment she felt toward Kellen, but a manifestation of her grief since Kellen looked so much like his late father, and shared so many of his personality traits.

"I'm sorry. That must have hurt. It must still hurt."

He swallowed, amazed at how perceptive Brigit was. Indeed, even as a thirty-six-year-old man, he was still hurt by his mother's distance, even if he could admit he'd helped push her away by doing everything in his power to confirm her low opinion of him.

Brigit was saying, "Surely since your accident, she's been supportive of you."

Pain, deep and unexpected, lanced his chest. “She’s been…busy.”

So busy doing whatever it was she did that she hadn’t been able to fly to Switzerland to be by his side at the hospital after his accident. Or after any of his many operations. Or at the chalet as he’d begun the grueling process of rehabilitation. She’d been so busy that, even after he made the long, transatlantic flight, she hadn’t been able to come to the airport to welcome him home.

He sipped his wine, which seemed to sour in his mouth.

“I’m sorry.”

He glanced over at Brigit. “For?”

“It took me a long time to figure out that my father’s shortcomings have nothing to do with me.”

“I’ve given her reasons—”

“No,” Brigit said, that one syllable brooking no argument. “Regardless of what you’ve done and how you’ve acted, your mother should have been there for you, Kellen.”

They sat in silence as the sun began to set. Words weren’t necessary. He liked that about her. Most of the women he knew would have become agitated, feeling ignored. Brigit merely sipped her wine, seeming to appreciate the view and the calming sound of the ocean as much as he did.

The inn's long shadow crept steadily over the beach as the sun began its descent. Kellen had drunk two glasses of wine. The alcohol hadn't calmed him as much as Brigit's company had. Just under half a bottle remained, but he knew it was pointless to ask her to stay for another round. The day was ending.

So, before she could say it, he announced, "It's time to call it a night."

"I was thinking the same thing," she replied, rising to her feet. She touched his shoulder. "But this…this was nice."

This as in the wine? Or was she referring to the evening off? Or spending time with him? He wanted to pin her down, but stopped himself from asking what she meant.

She had loaded up the tray and disappeared inside even before he managed to stand. By the time he reached the door, however, she was back. His muscles were stiff from sitting. His recent inactivity certainly hadn't helped. As a result, his leg was uncooperative, disobeying his brain's commands. He didn't bother trying to camouflage his discomfort or ungainliness as he moved inside. It was what it was.

"Own it and move forward," he murmured. His new mantra.

He hadn't intended the words to be loud enough for her to hear. Her brows drew together.

"What did you say?"

"Giving myself a pep talk." Half his mouth rose in a smile. "Someone recently told me something similar."

"She sounds smart," Brigit said lightly, stepping close and putting one of her arms around his waist for support.

Her fingers grazed his side before settling on his hip. He swore their heat radiated through the nylon fabric of his track pants. But what really grabbed his libido's attention was the way the side of her breast pressed against his ribs. Firm but surprisingly soft at the same time, much like the woman herself.

"She is," he murmured, dipping his head to

whisper the words against her ear. "And she knows it."

Brigit was a relatively small woman, but her large-and-in-charge personality made it impossible to consider her delicate. It was her power that appealed to him even more than the curve of her cheekbones or her dark-lashed blue eyes.

The air in the apartment was cool and humidity-free. But Kellen felt hot. He burned with sudden awareness. Long-dormant needs were now fully revived. Did she feel it, too? He recalled the kiss they'd shared on the deck just a week earlier. He'd forced it from his mind, told himself that he'd imagined the passion that had flared between them. What would a woman want with someone like him? *Fool*, he berated himself. But there was no escaping the truth. It burned inside him now—stronger, bolder, hotter. His breath hitched.

"Are you okay?" she asked.

He'd been hoping to work his way in that direction, but with her staring up at him, he was lost.

"No. I'm not okay."

"Maybe the wine wasn't such a good idea. Let's get you off your feet."

"Yes, let's," he murmured, although he doubted they had in mind the same idea for how to accomplish that.

His ardor cooled substantially when he spotted Joe sitting on the couch in the living room. The other man was watching television, a bottle of water in one hand and a bowl of popcorn in his lap. He glanced up as Kellen and Brigit staggered into view.

"Everything okay?" He set the bowl aside and wiped his hands on his T-shirt as he rose to his feet.

"What are you doing here?" Kellen asked.

"Lou ate some oysters that didn't agree with him, so we decided to call it a night."

"That's too bad," Brigit said. "For both of you."

Joe shrugged. "I didn't mind. The band sucked. Let me give you a hand." He started forward, but Brigit waved him off.

"I've got him. He's just a little stiff."

Indeed he was, though not how she meant.

She whispered to Kellen, "We wouldn't want him smelling wine on your breath."

Kellen nearly chuckled at that, but managed to keep a straight face.

"How's the leg tonight, Mr. F? Is it spasming again?"

"A little." He grunted before admitting, "It's my own damned fault."

Joe's brows shot up in surprise at his admission. Kellen glanced at Brigit, expecting to find a similar expression on her face. But she looked—what?—satisfied, pleased.

Taking total responsibility, he added, "I'm paying the price for all of my laziness. You've been doing your damnedest to help me, Joe. I haven't been a very good patient. That's going to change."

"Physical therapy at the usual time tomorrow?" Joe asked, his expression hopeful.

"No. First thing in the morning. Maybe we can add a second therapy session in the afternoon." Kellen swallowed, his gaze shifting to Brigit. "I'm not going to give up."

CHAPTER NINE

BRIGIT SLIPPED FROM bed even before her alarm went off the following morning. She hadn't slept well. Even though she'd dropped off not long after her head hit the pillow, she'd startled awake just after two and hadn't been able to fall back to sleep.

She wanted to blame the wine. But she knew it was the man. Kellen had her tied in knots.

It wasn't merely physical attraction causing her concern. That she could deal with, however inconvenient she might find it given their current living arrangement. Her ex had been Hollywood handsome with a former marine's hard body to match. It still galled her to admit that his good looks had blinded her to his controlling personality until after their wedding. What she had written off as overzealous courtesy while they were dating became rigid perimeters that had defined

daily life. If she'd needed something from the
store, Scott had insisted on going out for it. If a
package needed to be mailed, he had been the
one who took it to the post office. On and on
it had gone, until her life had been reduced to
what went on inside her home. And even there
she'd had no say. Everything from the paint col
ors to the style of curtains to the cleaning prod
ucts used—Scott had decided them all.

My way or the highway.

Scott actually had told her that once, before
their marriage, when they'd been settling a dis
agreement over their choice of reception venues
Foolishly, she'd thought he'd been kidding.

Kellen had a similar hard edge to him. He
could be stubborn. But he also could admit when
he was wrong.

Just when she'd been ready to write him off as
shallow and self-pitying, he'd surprised her. The
man wasn't as superficial as she'd assumed. In
addition to being sexually attracted to him, Bri
git had actually begun to like him.

She thought of the glimpses into his private
life that he'd allowed her the previous evening

Apparently, even before the accident his world hadn't been perfect. God knew, it was easier to think of him as spoiled, pampered and self-indulgent, but after what he'd told her, it was clear the silver spoon he'd been born with had tarnished over time.

Like Brigit, he'd grown up without a father. Worse, at least to her way of thinking, he had known and loved his father, only to have illness snatch him away. Meanwhile, Kellen's mother hadn't been there for him.

Hard to please. Hard to live with. Hard to love.

Brigit found Kellen's blunt description of his relationship with his only surviving parent sad. If someone were to ask Brigit to describe her mom, the words on the tip of her tongue would be loving, devoted and dependable. Delia Wright always had made Brigit feel safe. Even as an adult, Brigit knew she could rely on her mother, which was why when she'd finally left Scott that was where she'd gone. Home to her mom, where she'd been welcomed with open arms and gently chastised for not coming sooner.

Kellen had come home to…a resort.

Outside her room, Brigit could hear someone moving around. She figured it would be Joe, getting ready to start his day. She wondered when Kellen would rise. He'd claimed he wanted to start his physical therapy first thing. His resoluteness the night before had seemed sincere but would he?

She was still wearing her favorite UConn T-shirt and pair of plaid boxer shorts when a light tap sounded at the door. Joe probably needed some of his things from the dresser they were sharing.

"Just a sec," she called. While her outfit was hardly provocative, she wasn't wearing a bra and the shorts barely covered the tops of her thighs. She pulled on a robe and loosely belted it for modesty's sake.

It wasn't Joe who stood in the hallway, but Kellen. Her heart executed a funny tuck and roll at the sight of him. Some of his hair stuck up on his crown and his jaw was shadowed in stubble. If she had to guess, she'd say he'd just gotten out of bed. Her heart somersaulted a second time at she pictured him there, tucked amid the blankets wearing…

"Good morning." His voice was roughened by sleep, but his gaze was alert as it did a quick view of her body.

Brigit shivered even as her blood heated.

"Good morning. You're up early," she told him.

"I couldn't sleep."

Oh? What had kept him awake? She felt like an idiot for briefly hoping it had been thoughts of her.

"Eager to get to work with Joe?"

He eyed her for a moment. "Sure."

Kellen tucked his hands into the pockets of his track pants. They were black with a trio of white stripes down the sides of both legs. But what snagged her attention was his T-shirt. She was wearing its twin.

"Nice shirt."

He glanced down, then back at her. "Thanks."

At his confused expression, she pulled the lapels of her robe open to show him her tee. The view provided far more than mere clarity, how-

ever. Her taut nipples strained against the fabric
beneath the university's logo.

"UConn never looked so good," he murmured.

The loosened belt rode low on her hips. Kellen
hooked his finger over the spot where it tied. His
fingertip gently scored her belly through the thin
cotton of her shorts. A gentle tug was all it took
to release the tie completely. The sash fell to the
floor, taking common sense with it. When his
gaze detoured to her bare legs, she felt her flesh
once again prickle with desire.

Brigit hadn't been with a man since her divorce.
For that matter, she'd been on only a couple dates
in all that time, both set up by her well-mean-
ing big sister. On the island, which was largely
populated with tourists for much of the year, i
was easy to dodge any sort of intimacy. Her job
kept her busy for most of her waking hours, and
any men she met were either guests at the resort
which put them off-limits, or guests at anothe
resort, and as such in town for only a brief time

When it came to Kellen, she was playing with
fire, and the look in his eyes told her he was only
too happy to provide the kindling. Well, one o

them needed to be smart and act like an adult rather than a sex-crazed teen. Brigit figured that role fell to her.

She had the most to lose, after all. He owned the resort. He was her boss. He wasn't going to stay on the island any longer than it took him to recover. Meanwhile, this was her career, her livelihood, her home. It was her heart, a soft voice whispered.

She swallowed and pushed that thought aside. Her heart was in no danger, she told herself. Besides, Kellen needed her. He'd told her so the previous night. And what he needed—what they *both* needed—was for her to remain levelheaded. So she tugged the robe's lapels together and folded her arms over her breasts.

"Is there something you needed from me?"

She intended the question to be polite rather than provocative, but given the interest that flared in his eyes, she had a pretty good idea in which direction his mind had veered. God help them, hers wanted to follow.

Be professional, she reminded herself. *Be sensible.*

Apparently he had conducted a similar internal pep talk, because he glanced away and replied, "I just wanted to let you know that I'm going to skip morning coffee on the deck."

Disappointment settled like a barbell in her stomach. It was silly to look forward to that hour or so while they sat together watching the sun rise. Half the time, they didn't even speak.

Half "Oh?"

"I decided to get the torture over first thing." A rueful grin accompanied the words.

"Ah. And here I thought maybe you had decided to heed his advice and take up green tea," she quipped, keeping their banter light and friendly.

"Let's not get carried away."

Joe picked that moment to amble down the hall. He was dressed in the same clothes he'd been wearing the day before, although his hair was damp from a shower. He held a half-eaten apple in one hand.

"I see I don't need to wake up either of you." He studied Kellen then. "Ready to be pushed Mr. F?"

Kellen sobered, his expression just this side of fierce when he replied, "Bring it on."

"That's the attitude I was hoping for. I thought we'd start with some basic stretching exercises before moving on to the strengthening ones." Joe's gaze slid to Brigit then. "We can start in the living room with some tension bands and the medicine ball, but eventually we'll require some of the equipment in here."

"Of course. Not a problem. Give me twenty minutes to shower, dress and grab my things, and the room is all yours." She sent Kellen what she hoped was an encouraging smile. "Good luck."

Later that day, Kellen sat alone at a table in the dining room. He was tired, sore, sleepy even, given his restless night. But he'd resisted the urge to lie down. Not only because he'd promised to turn over a new leaf, but because Brigit had claimed she would join him for lunch.

Unfortunately, she had yet to come and sit down. He'd eaten half of his Joe-approved Waldorf salad when he heard a familiar voice call his name.

"Kellen Faust, as I live and breathe."

He turned to find Jennifer Cherville crossing to his table. At one time the two of them had been an item. They'd dated throughout college. Not surprisingly, after graduation, Jennifer had expected an engagement ring. Kellen, meanwhile, had purchased a new pair of skis and booked a flight to Switzerland. Where she'd wanted to settle down, preferably in Charleston, and start producing little Kellens, he'd wanted to defy death on the slopes. How differently his life might be now if she'd gotten her way. Even so, he had no regrets.

She wasn't the sort of woman he wanted to wake up to every morning. A fiercely determined black-haired beauty came to mind.

When Jennifer reached his table, he tried to rise.

"No, no. You poor thing. Don't get up." She pressed her hand to his shoulder and then leaned down to air-kiss his cheeks. "I heard you were back. Courtney—you remember Courtney Dobson?" Before he could even nod, Jennifer was saying, "She and I stopped at the club the other night for dinner and ran into your mother and father."

"Stepfather," he corrected thinly.

"Anyway, she mentioned you were home." Jennifer tipped her head sideways and her tone turned syrupy with sympathy. "How are you?"

"I'm fine."

"Aww, Kellen. So brave."

She offered a patronizing smile while he gritted his teeth. Just a week earlier, he would have asked if she had come to the island to gawk at the invalid. He would have treated her rudely and been insufferable. Unlike Brigit, who had called him on the carpet for his bad behavior, Jennifer would have reacted with teary eyes and run away.

"Did you get the flowers I sent?" she asked.

"Flowers?"

"Stargazer lilies," she added, as if that would mean something to him. He didn't know a daisy from a tulip. "I had them delivered to the hospital after your accident."

He recalled the assortment of bouquets, plants and get-well cards that had lined the surfaces in his room, although who had sent what escaped him now. But he nodded anyway.

"Thank you." His manners had been rusty, but the more he used them, the easier it became. So, he added, "That was kind of you."

"It was the least I could do. I was very worried about you. I'm still very worried about you, Kellen. If there's anything I can do to help. *Anything*. Just ask."

What to say to that? He settled on repeating, "That's kind of you."

She leaned closer and said, "You know, I've never quite gotten over you."

"Jen—"

"All these years, and I still find myself hoping…"

He'd never made any promises, but after four years of dating, it was understandable that she'd made assumptions. He regretted that.

And he regretted that, just as Jen made her provocative admission, Brigit showed up at their table. Her gaze slid from Kellen to Jennifer and back, one brow arched. But he'd be damned if he could tell what she was thinking.

"Should I bring over another chair?" she asked politely.

Jennifer glanced at her, apparently noted the logo on the shirt and, before Kellen could say anything, replied, "There's no need for that. The table already has two chairs."

"Yes, but the free one is taken."

"By whom?" Jennifer asked, her tone affronted. She straightened. In heels, she was as tall as Kellen, and so she towered over Brigit, making it all the easier to look down her surgically improved nose. Kellen knew her parents had given her rhinoplasty for her twenty-first birthday.

"Me." Brigit dropped into it, making a show of folding the cloth napkin over her lap.

Jennifer transferred her outraged glare from Brigit to Kellen. Not sure what else to do, he made introductions.

"Brigit Wright, this is Jennifer Cherville. Jen, Brigit."

"Brigit, hmm. I see that you work here." Jennifer pointed to the logo on Brigit's shirt.

"That's right. I've managed Faust Haven for the past five years."

"That's nice." Jen's tone was condescending. "Kellen and I go back more than a decade. We were college sweethearts."

"That's nice," Brigit parroted, using the same mocking tone.

Kellen did his best to keep a straight face. Meanwhile, Jen's eyes narrowed.

"Do you mind? Kellen and I were having a private conversation."

"Shall I leave you alone?" Brigit asked him.

"No. We had a lunch date." He shifted his gaze to Jennifer. "Look, Jen. I appreciate your concern, but there's no need for it. I may not be fine, but I am getting better."

"Yes, about that. Your mother told me you were back in Charleston to see another specialist. She also mentioned all of the other medical opinions you've already received."

"Then I'm sure you know my dancing days are over," he replied lightly, surprised by the absence of bitterness. As Brigit had noted when making her point mere days earlier, he wasn't likely to take up the tango or cha-cha or any number of ballroom staples. Surprisingly, he was okay with that. More of the gratitude he should have been feeling all along for simply being alive made an appearance.

Jennifer, however, wailed, “Oh, Kellen! Don’t say such things. Don’t even think them!”

“Shall I leave you alone?” Brigit asked again. Her dry tone told him exactly what she thought of the other woman’s theatrics.

“There’s no need. Jen won’t be staying.” He transferred his gaze back to the statuesque blonde. “I appreciate your concern, but it’s not necessary. Really.”

She pursed her lips and nodded. He could tell she didn’t quite believe him. “If you change your mind, Daddy knows an orthopedic surgeon at Johns Hopkins. Dr. Taft is relatively young, but Daddy says he’s excellent at what he does. A true visionary when it comes to trying new treatment protocols. A lot of professional athletes seek him out after they suffer what are considered career-ending injuries. He can perform miracles.”

For a second time, she leaned over to kiss his cheek. This time, however, her lips made contact. After shooting a pointed look at Brigit, she left.

"So, are you going to call him?"

"Who?" Kellen asked before taking a sip of his ice water.

"The miracle worker your girlfriend mentioned."

He nearly spat out the water.

"First, Jen is not my girlfriend. We dated. Past tense. It was a long time ago."

Brigit shrugged. "And second?"

"Second, no, I'm not going to call him. No more doctors, no more opinions."

"Oh?"

"The diagnosis would be the same. My prognosis, however, well, that's up to me."

"Yes, it is."

Brigit smiled. She looked satisfied, smug. Something about her was different. He studied her closely trying to figure out exactly what it was. Her attire was the same, a uniform top that wasn't intended to draw attention to her figure. Her hair was the same, black curls pulled back in their usual ponytail, which swung like a pendulum between her shoulder blades whenever she walked. Her makeup was minimal, just the barest hint of mascara on her long lashes and no kind of foundation, or whatever it was called, to cover up her freckles.

Some people might call her looks average. Pretty, but certainly not stunning. Kellen might have been one of them if he hadn't glimpsed the determination and steel beneath her relatively nondescript facade. To him, Brigit was beautiful, and growing more so with each new thing he learned about her.

"Why are you looking at me that way?"

"No reason," he lied, even as the truth buzzed around inside him like an out-of-control bee.

For the first time in his life, he was in danger of falling in love.

CHAPTER TEN

BRIGIT FOUND THE cane while she was down in the storage area rummaging around for a vase to hold more seashells. It was black with a curved and ornately carved handle inlaid with mother-of-pearl.

She brought the handle closer to study the figure carved into it. Was that a seahorse? The tail seemed wrong. Wider and scaly, shaped more like a snake's with a fish's fin at the end. Regardless, she knew who it had belonged to: Kellen's grandfather.

As such, she knew he would welcome its return, the timing of which was perfect since other than the piece of driftwood, he still didn't have a replacement for the one that had broken.

She waited until dinnertime to give it to him. It wasn't exactly a gift, since technically it already belonged to him. But she wrapped it up anyway—as best as one could wrap a cane—and was excited to see his reaction when he opened it.

Instead of eating in the dining room, she suggested they dine on the sprawling deck just outside it. Diners were sparse outdoors this evening. Not only was it hot, but the sky had turned gray. A storm was forecast—thunder, lightning and the works—for later in the evening.

"Are you sure you want to eat out here?" Kellen asked a second time after a gust of wind whipped the napkin right off her lap.

"If the breeze picks up any more we can move inside, but I prefer it out here." The draft rustled his hair and she was tempted to reach across the table and smooth it down. Instead, she turned her attention to the ocean, where frothy waves churned to shore. "Mother Nature's going to be putting on quite the show later."

"That's one way to put it," he replied. "You sound like you're looking forward to it."

"I like storms," she admitted. "Especially when I'm indoors, safe and dry. I always have, except when—"

"Except when?" he prompted.

"For a brief time in my twenties," she hedged. While married to Scott, a sense of security had eluded her no matter what the weather.

"Why then?" he asked. "What about that time made you dislike storms?"

She shook her head.

"You would have been married then." His brows rose. "Right?"

"What about you? How do you feel about storms?" she diverted.

To her surprise, he snapped his fingers and shook his head. "I thought I had you."

"What do you mean?"

"I thought you'd open up a little, maybe even tell me some of your deep, dark secrets."

"I have no secrets to tell," she lied. "Deep, dark or otherwise."

He made a humming sound. "If you did, would you share them with me?"

The question had her swallowing. Something was happening between them, growing stronger just like the wind. A storm was brewing in more ways than one. It left her with that same feeling of anticipation rather than fear.

"I'd have to be able to trust you," she said slowly.

"And you don't now?"

"I'm starting to."

It was an honest answer, but she thought he might object to it. He was a man accustomed to having his wants and needs met instantly. Or at least he had been. Once again, he proved to be changing, improving more than physically.

"I'll work harder then."

He shifted in his seat and the driftwood cane slid along the table's edge before falling to the deck.

"That reminds me," she told him as she bent to retrieve it. "I have something for you."

"Like a gift."

"Like a surprise."

"Even better," he replied on a grin.

Their hands touched as she handed back the walking stick. A simple brush of skin that had the same effect as a lighted match dropped on kindling. His gaze lingered on her mouth. She forced herself to break contact and reach for her cellphone.

"I just need to make a quick call."

"Now? After you got me all worked up?" He grinned. "Over a surprise, I mean."

"The call relates to the surprise."

She tapped Danny's number into her cell. The young bellman answered immediately since he'd been expecting her call.

"Ready." That was all Brigit said before hanging up.

"Very cryptic," Kellen murmured. "You have me intrigued."

He changed his tune as soon as Danny came onto the deck carrying the wrapped cane.

"Gee. I wonder what it could be," he said dryly as he took the item from the bellboy, who returned inside.

"Looks can be deceiving."

"Isn't that the truth," he replied with feeling. "Should I open it now?"

"Unless you want to continue the suspense."

He ripped off the paper, which Brigit then

balled up in a wad so it wouldn't be whisked off by the wind.

"A cane! Who knew?"

"Not just any cane. This one belonged to your grandfather."

Kellen's grin faltered and his gaze lowered to the item in his hands. He turned it over, his expression became reverent. "I remember this thing. Granddad didn't need a cane to walk, but a friend of his had traveled to Greece and brought it back for him."

"So that creature carved on the handle, it's part of Greek mythology?"

Kellen nodded. "A hippocampus. Where did you find it?"

"In the storage room. I was looking for a vase earlier today when I stumbled across it. There might be other personal effects of his in there if you want to have a look sometime."

"I will." He glanced over at her then. "Thank you."

Kellen rested his head against the side of the tub and let the pulsating water soothe his screaming muscles. After a full three weeks of relentless torture, he'd thought Joe might give him the weekend off, or at least ease up on the grueling routine. But he hadn't. If anything, Saturday's sessions had been more intense than ever. And the one this morning? Nothing short of merciless.

"Let me know if you can't handle it," Joe had said mildly before cranking up the resistance on the stationary bike.

Kellen swore the therapist had only made the offer to appeal to his boss's stubborn streak. Regardless, the trick had worked. Whatever Joe had dished out, Kellen had taken and then come back for seconds. He was paying for his pride now.

Still, he thought he was making headway. As sore as they were, the muscles in his thigh and calf didn't seem quite so rigid or as hard to control when he walked. He still leaned heavily on his cane, but his leg was starting to feel more stable. When he walked, he no longer worried that his mangled knee would give out or lock up and cause him to fall. All this after less than a month.

He berated himself for not applying himself with such vigor earlier. Who knew what progress he might have made by now if he had?

Or if he'd come to the island sooner, to Faust Haven. He gave the place some of the credit for the turnaround in his condition. And Brigit, of course. No, Brigit most of all. She'd offered him just the kick in the pants he'd needed to start living again rather than merely existing. He wasn't sure how to repay her. But repay her he would.

He recalled the severance papers he'd had his lawyer draw up. They ensured that Brigit would be well-compensated for not only her years of service, but her assistance with his recovery. But they weren't the repayment he had in mind. Indeed, Kellen hadn't thought of the papers in weeks. Nor did he want to think of them now, much less to think of Brigit leaving the resort. Leaving him. More so than any other time in his life, his life seemed in flux, his future far from determined.

Things Kellen had thought he'd wanted no longer mattered. Things he'd never thought would appeal to him suddenly did. He wasn't sure how, but Brigit figured into the chaos. Somehow, she figured into his future.

Twenty minutes later, he sat up in the tub and turned off the jets. The water had grown cool and Kellen wanted to get out. Unfortunately, that wasn't a feat he could manage without some assistance. He hollered for Joe three times before he finally heard footsteps outside the door.

"Get in here, already," he shouted. "I'm turning into a prune."

But it wasn't the physical therapist who answered. It was Brigit.

Her tone was tentative when she told him, "Um, Joe isn't here."

"What do you mean, Joe isn't here? Where did he go?"

"I'm not sure, but he's not in the apartment. I just stopped in to grab a yogurt when I heard you calling. I can go look for him, if you'd like?" she offered.

Who knew how long that would take? In the meantime, Kellen wanted out of the tub.

"That's all right. I can…I can do this," he said

and reached to unplug the stopper. Water began to glug down the drain.

"Do what?" She sounded alarmed. "What are you going to do, Kellen?"

"I'm going to get out of the tub."

"I think you should wait for Joe." The door muffled her reply, but he still heard the concern in her tone.

Meanwhile, the water was down from the middle of his chest to his belly. Gooseflesh prickled his skin. He wasn't going to wait. "I'll be careful," he promised.

Standing up was going to be difficult, but the real challenge would be swinging his leg over the side of the tub. One way or another, he would have to balance momentarily on his bad leg. After weeks of strengthening exercises, would his knee hold?

Only one way to find out. Kellen grabbed the side of the tub, rolled onto one side and wedged his good knee beneath his body. The water that remained in the tub sloshed around his hips.

"Kellen!" Brigit shouted. "What are you doing?"

"Trying to stand."

"No! Absolutely not. Do you hear me? You need to sit back down and wait for Joe."

The same pride that had pushed him these past few weeks during his physical therapy sessions reasserted itself. Kellen wasn't going to sit down. He wasn't going to wait. He was going to get up and get out of the tub under his own steam.

With both arms over the side of the tub, he pushed to his knees. Barely six inches of water remained in the tub. He watched as a funnel formed over the drain, and debated the wisdom of waiting until the rest of it was gone.

"Kellen!"

"I'm fine. I can do this," he told her, hoping to convince them both.

Brigit wasn't buying it. "Cover up because I'm coming in," she called a moment before he heard the doorknob jiggle.

What the…? She wouldn't. But she would. And she did. He had just enough time to yank the towel off the bar before she barged in with her eyes pinched closed and one hand out in front of her, apparently to ensure she didn't run into anything.

"Are you decent?" she asked. "Can I open my eyes?"

He was resting on the heels of his feet with the towel thrown over his lap. The ends on either side floated in the remaining few inches of water. Even though he was sufficiently covered, he still felt exposed. He was stronger, heavier than he'd been when she'd seen him shirtless that first day at the resort, but he was a long way from his once-chiseled physique.

He answered honestly. "I'd rather you didn't see me like this, Brigit."

Her eyes opened, her gaze focused on his face. "See you like what, Kellen?" Even though she hadn't looked down, she said, "You're sufficiently covered."

"That's not what I mean. I used to be…a lot more physically fit than this."

"You look pretty good to me, especially for someone on the mend."

Her tone was matter-of-fact, but a blush crept up her cheeks.

The sight of her flushed face assuaged his ego.

"Yeah?"

She nodded.

"You look better than pretty good to me," he said softly. "You're beautiful, Brigit. Inside and out. So strong."

"Not many men appreciate strength in a woman," she said quietly.

"Well, I do."

The last of the water gurgled down the drain, breaking the spell.

"Can you grab my bathrobe from the hook?"

He pointed to where it hung and she handed it to him. While she turned her back to him, he pushed the soggy towel aside, shrugged into the robe and secured its belt.

"I'm ready," he told her as he got back up on his knees, distributing more of his weight to the good one to lessen the pain.

She turned around and studied him for a moment, tapping one finger against her lips. Nothing about her pose was provocative, nor were her words when she told him, "I think I need to get in there with you."

That didn't stop his libido from firing to life. Even as he was trying to wrestle his desire into submission, she was toeing off her shoes and stepping into the tub.

"Let me just get behind you," she said, slipping around so that she was all but straddling his back.

He swallowed thickly, wishing their positions were reversed. Wishing she wasn't fully clothed, but naked like he was under the robe, her skin slick and slippery from soap and water.

He groaned.

"Are you in pain?" she asked.

Oh, he was in pain all right. But Kellen shook his head. "Let's get this over with."

"So impatient," she muttered.

"You have no idea," he muttered back.

She bent over and slipped her hands under his arms. She wasn't wearing her usual ponytail so some of her hair fell forward and tickled the side of his face. He inhaled deeply as her scent enveloped him.

"Let's get you into a standing position. On the count of three, okay?"

"Mm-hmm." He inhaled again.

"One…two…three."

Her grip was surprisingly strong. Added to his effort, he managed to push up so that one foot was planted firmly on the bottom of the tub. He braced both of his hands on his thigh. With her help, he was able to get his bad leg to cooperate. Finally, he was standing.

Brigit's hands were no longer under Kellen's arms. Now, they were resting on his waist just above the robe's sash. It would be so easy for her to unfasten it and reach beneath it, where she would find his body eager and more than ready. Despite his best efforts to stop it, a fantasy formed of her doing just that. He found himself almost wishing for the cool water that had been drained from the tub. Anything to shock him back to his senses.

"Okay, now I want you to sit on the edge of the tub. I'm going to get out. Then I'll help you swing your legs over the side." She stepped over the edge as he lowered onto it. "Ready?" she asked.

He offered a jerky nod and dutifully followed

ıer instructions, hoping the robe would hide his ırousal as she helped him lift his legs over the ide. He needed to think of something else. One of his elementary school history teachers had nade Kellen write out the preamble to the US Constitution forty times for talking in class. As uch he had it committed to memory. He began o recite it in his head. Anything to get his mind ff sex.

We the people of the United States, in order to orm a more perfect union...

Once his feet were planted on the tile floor, she ffered him her hands. Standing in front of him, er breasts were at mouth level. Kellen swal-owed.

...establish justice, insure domestic tranquil-y, provide for the common defense...

"Okay, now stand."

He started to straighten, shifting most of his veight to his good leg. Brigit gripped his hands nd smiled encouragement. How was it possible or this woman to tie him in knots and unravel is worries at the same time?

...promote the general welfare...

"You did it."

"With your help," he amended.

"We make a good team."

He nodded and leaned closer, lured by he scent. Distracted, it took him a moment to rea ize that she was backing up.

"Come on."

He took a step. Some water must have bee on the floor, because his foot started to slip. Th harder Kellen fought to maintain his balance, th more precarious his footing became on the slic tile. Brigit's eyes widened with concern and sh wrapped her arms around him just as he starte to go down.

The fall seemed to take place in slow motio He didn't go down with a crash as much as h slumped and wound up cushioned on her bod He stared down into a pair of blue eyes tha looked as surprised as he felt.

"Are you okay?" he asked, shifting his weig so that his hip and good leg were on the floo His bad leg, however, remained draped acros both of hers, and his hands were braced on e ther side of her shoulders.

Brigit's lips twitched with a smile. "I think that's supposed to be my line."

If she could joke at a time like this, then surely she couldn't be injured. He commanded his jackhammering heart to slow, but it picked up speed as he became aware not only of how lovely she looked with her dark hair fanned out over the crisp white tile, but of their rather intimate pose. His chest was mere inches from the tips of her breasts, and his erection was pressed against her hip, growing harder by the minute. Even if he were still so inclined, there was no way to hide his desire now.

The preamble. The damned preamble. What came next? Something about blessings.

...And secure the blessings of liberty to ourselves and our posterity...

Brigit was no longer smiling. Her expression had switched to solemn, and the crystal-blue eyes that were regarding him had turned almost opaque. Was she feeling it, too? All of that pent-up need that was just begging to be satisfied?

He was fighting a losing battle, and he knew it.

...do ordain and establish this Constitution fo the United States of America.

He finished the words in a rush in his head Aloud, he muttered, "To hell with it."

Watching her closely to gauge her mood, h lowered his head. He saw no protest, felt no re sistance. When their lips met, her lids drifte closed and he felt her arms come up around hi shoulders.

In the instant before he deepened the kiss, sound—half sigh, half moan—vibrated from he throat. Oh, yeah. She was every bit as turned o as he was.

Unfortunately, it was becoming clear h couldn't continue to brace himself above her fc much longer. As it was, his arms were beginnin to shake from the strain. Any minute now, the were going to give out on him. Even though h was still fifteen pounds shy of his usual weigh Kellen still worried that if he lowered his tors to hers he would be too heavy, especially sinc the tile floor beneath her offered none of the giv a mattress would.

He was just getting ready to suggest they tak

heir business elsewhere when he heard the shuf-
'ling of feet. They broke off the kiss and both
glanced toward the door. Joe stood at the threshold with his hands on his hips, doing his best to
uck away a grin.

"I see you didn't need my help getting out of
he tub after all, Mr. F."

CHAPTER ELEVEN

"GOING FOR YOUR WALK?" Kellen asked the fol
lowing evening as Brigit laced up her shoes.

She had changed into shorts and he took a mo
ment to admire her toned legs.

She glanced over. "That's right. I won't be gon
long. I'll challenge you and Joe to a game of gi
rummy when I get back."

It wasn't exactly what he wanted to hear. Sinc
their encounter in the bathroom the day befor
Kellen hadn't had a moment alone with he
Whether on the deck in the morning or sittin
in the living room just now, Joe was always wit
them. Three had definitely become a crowd.

"Mind if I go with you?"

Brigit blinked in surprise. "For a walk?"

"That's right."

"On the beach," she said slowly.

"That's where you usually walk, isn't it?"

She looked at Joe, who was in the kitchen making God only knew what with kale.

In exasperation, Kellen asked, “What? Do I need his permission?”

“No, I just… The sand is hard to walk on.”

“I’m up for the challenge. Unless you’d rather go by yourself,” he said.

“No. I don’t mind the company.” She smiled, glanced away, her expression oddly shy. “I just wanted to be sure Joe thought it was a good idea.”

The physical therapist grinned. “It’ll be more work walking through sand than on a boardwalk. You had a pretty intense workout tonight, Mr. F. Sure you’re feeling up to it?”

The only thing Kellen was certain of was that he wanted some time alone with Brigit. But he smiled and nodded. “I’m sure.”

His cane wasn’t much support since it kept sinking into the ground. But Brigit walked close by his side as they made their way to the beach. The going was slow and difficult. They used a well-worn path between the dunes that was free of vegetation. Once they were on the beach

proper, she pointed to the spot just shy of wher
the surf churned at the shore.

"It will be easier to walk down there. The san
is flat and hard. Of course, your feet might get
little wet from time to time."

"I'll chance it."

Once they reached the compacted, damp sand
walking was indeed much easier. Brigit dance
out of range to avoid rogue waves that lappe
ashore in their path. Kellen, however, had nei
ther the agility nor the coordination to do so
which meant his feet, shoes and all, were soo
drenched. He didn't care. Other than for his doc
tor appointment, this was the first time he'd bee
outside the resort since his arrival. He didn'
count sitting on the deck, where he'd been
spectator more than a participant.

"You're doing well," she commented.

"Thanks. I'm trying not to embarrass mysel
in front of you after yesterday's bathtub fiasco.

She pushed dark hair away from her face. He
smile was secretive, borderline sly, when she tol
him, "I don't know, I thought that turned ou
okay, all things considered."

"It ended before it began."

"That's not quite how I remember it."

"Yeah?" He recalled their kiss, the way their bodies had fitted together on the floor. She had a point. "Well, Joe's timing still sucks."

"I have to agree with you on that." She chuckled.

"In addition to being my physical therapist, he's starting to seem like a chaperone."

"Do I need one?"

For what seemed like the millionth time, Kellen found himself wondering where things would have led had he and Brigit not been interrupted. He knew where he'd *wanted* things to go.

"You might." He snagged her hand and stopped walking, forcing her to as well. "This is where, as your boss, I should apologize for my…forward behavior."

"Forward, hmm? Seemed horizontal to me."

Her lips quirked and he was tempted to kiss away the humor he spied there. But he had something to say, something important.

"I know the kind of reputation I have."

She was serious now as well. "I know it, too. I

read the stories, Kellen. Long before you arrived
on the island. In fact, before I ever took the job
here, I did some internet searches. I was curious
about the man I was going to work for."

"And?" he prompted.

"I'd like to say that I withheld judgment and
gave you the benefit of the doubt. After all, the
tabloids are notorious for making mountains
out of molehills or out of no hills, for that matter." She scrunched up her nose. "But I did make
some assumptions."

"Where there's smoke there's fire?" he asked,
his tone wry.

She nodded.

A five-alarm blaze in his case, Kellen thought.
He'd lived carelessly, living up to—or was that
down to?—his mother's low opinion of him.

"Let me guess," he began. "You thought I was
slacker, living off my trust fund instead of earning a living. That I partied seven days a week
surrounded by people as aimless, unambitiou
and self-involved as I was."

As he spoke, a wave splashed over their feet.
Brigit didn't try to avoid it this time. Even a

the water frothed around their ankles before receding, she seemed not to notice. He had her complete attention. The hems of his track pants were soaked and clinging to his ankles. Some of the sand under his feet slipped away. But that wasn't why he felt off balance as he watched Brigit closely and tried to gauge her reaction. What she thought of him…it mattered. More than it had ever mattered with anyone else before.

"Was I wrong?" she asked slowly.

"No. Not in the least." It was a hard thing to admit, especially to this woman, for whom he was starting to develop such serious feelings. Yet the admission was cathartic at the same time. "I'm not proud of it, but I was all those things and more."

"Was." She nodded and squeezed his hand. "I like the sound of that."

"Do you?"

"Yes."

"I like the sound of it, too. I have changed, Brigit. I want to be sure you know that. It's important to me."

She studied him, wide blue eyes unblinking
"Why? Why is that so important?"

His emotions were churning as forcefully a
the surf. "It just is. Your opinion matters to me
I've never met anyone quite like you."

"I'm…flattered."

His heart sank. It wasn't exactly what he'
hoped to hear.

He lowered his head, his tone beseeching as h
pressed, "Is that all you are? I could have swor
you felt…something more the other day."

"You're my boss, Kellen. I work for you."

"What if you didn't?" He wasn't thinking abou
the severance package, although he needed t
tell her about it at some point. But now wasn'
the time. Besides, he rationalized, maybe ther
would continue to be a position for her at Faus
Haven. So much was in flux, not the least o
which were his emotions. But the resort's man
agement wasn't the point of this conversatio
anyway. So he changed tactics. "Tell me you'r
not attracted to me."

She issued a strangled laugh. "You know tha
I am."

"But?"

"I'm not in the market for a relationship."

Kellen wasn't sure he was either. Other than with Jennifer, he'd never maintained a serious, long-term bond with a woman. He suspected her reasons were not quite as shallow as his. "Your ex-husband really did a number on you."

"He did." The words came out so softly that even though he was bending close, Kellen was barely able to hear them.

"Want to talk about it?" he asked. Brigit's eyes widened. She wasn't able to camouflage her astonishment. He chuckled drily. "I'm as surprised as you are, but over the past few weeks, I think I've become a better listener."

And wasn't that the truth, he marveled. The evolution of Kellen Faust continued, and the woman standing next to him had played a huge role in his personal growth.

"It's not something I like to remember, much less talk about."

"I get it. No problem." Disappointed, he nodded anyway. The few snippets of information she'd told Kellen about her ex, the more curious he became. Still, he knew better than to press.

They started to walk again. Their fingers were still loosely knit together. She broke the contac to bend down and pick up a shell. Realizing i was broken, she tossed it back into the ocean Then she reached for Kellen's hand again.

"Scott was a marine. And a good friend of my sister's husband's. That's how we met. Scott was the best man at Mitch and Robbie's wedding, and I was the maid of honor. We had a whirlwind courtship and, six months later..." She held up one hand. "We got married. My mom though it was too soon. I was just finishing up college She wanted me to experience a little more of life before I settled down. I think she worried I was looking for a father figure, since my dad had never been in the picture."

Kellen could see her mother's point. But he held his tongue and waited for Brigit to continue

"While we were dating he was the perfec gentleman. He opened doors for me. If I was cold, he gave me his coat. When we went out to eat at a restaurant, he insisted on ordering my meals. When we went to the movies, he picked the feature. Now I see those last couple things as red flags, but back then?" Her shoulders lifted. "I thought of them as old-fashioned chivalry. I thought I was marrying the man of my dreams," she said quietly. "Boy, was I wrong."

"What happened?"

"You know, I've asked myself that same thing a million times." Brigit frowned. "I mean, how come I didn't see it coming? All I know is that the solicitous guy I dated and the controlling man I married were like Dr. Jekyll and Mr. Hyde."

Kellen gripped the walking stick with almost painful force. "Did he…did he hurt you?"

"Physically? No, not really. I mean, he grabbed me by the shoulders a few times and gave me a shake, but he never punched me or anything like that. But emotionally…"

It took her a moment to go on. In that time Kellen's blood ran cold.

"Everything in our house had to be just so. Canned goods had to be lined up, but not touching, with labels facing out. Towels were folded a specific way and then placed in the linen closet

so that you could see rolled edge rather than the
individual layers. Anything that was placed in
the dishwasher had to be thoroughly rinsed first.
The smallest smudge of food and I was in for a
lecture. I know what you're thinking."

"I doubt it."

"A lecture. What's the big deal? But after a
while his words were like drips of water on stone.
They wore away at me. I began to doubt myself."

She picked up another shell. Discarded it as
well. Hand in hand they continued to walk. And
she went on with what he knew had to be a pain
ful recitation of her past.

"The obsessive behavior was annoying and a
little freaky, but then he started to get paranoid.
He took away my cell phone, and I had to ask
permission to use the landline. It was for my
own good, he told me. He said I was too naive.
I failed to see other people's true motives." Her
laughter was harsh. "He had a point. I mean,
didn't see him for what he was until we were le
gally bound together."

Kellen was hardly an expert on matrimony
but what Brigit was describing was a prison sen

tence, not a marriage. Her husband had been her jailer. Kellen recalled what she'd said earlier about her ex not wanting her to work. No wonder. It was easier to control someone who had no money of her own, no outside contacts. He squeezed her fingers. "That wasn't your fault."

"I know. Now."

She didn't hesitate with her response, which told Kellen that in the five years since her divorce, she had meticulously sorted through her baggage and lightened the load considerably. He admired her for that.

"But at the time you weren't so sure."

"No. And so, yeah, I did blame myself. All those drips of water, you know. When Scott got mad or upset, it was always because of something I'd done or had failed to do."

"Which made his bad mood your problem." The assessment hit a little too close to home for Kellen, since he'd lashed out at everyone around him after his accident. Still, he wanted to believe his behavior had never bordered on abusive.

"Don't," she said softly.

"What?"

"Don't compare yourself to him. You're not the least bit similar."

"I appreciate the reassurance, believe me, but I know I was a jerk to be around."

"Oh, totally," she agreed without compunction. "But you were still nothing like Scott. You never waged psychological warfare on me or the other people around you. That was his tactic, his specialty. He blamed me for his foul moods so often that I started to believe it myself." A groove had formed between her eyebrows. "It didn't hurt that Scott was a master at making me feel worthless and useless and, worst of all, helpless."

Kellen had never done that. Even at his most obnoxious, he'd never made the people around him feel inferior. As much as he regretted the way he'd been acting, at least he had that in his favor.

"What did your family say?"

"They didn't say anything because they didn't know."

"You didn't go to them?" He couldn't hide his surprise. From everything she'd told him about her mother and sister, it had seemed a safe assumption that she would turn to them in her time of need.

But Brigit was saying, "How could I tell my mom that she had been right about Scott, when she was telling me how happy she was that I hadn't listened to her?" She shook her head. "He was on his best behavior around her. He was on his best behavior around my sister and brother-in-law. I was the only one who saw the real Scott. And he had me half convinced I was imagining things."

"But you got out."

"It took me four years to do it, but yes. I got out. By then my brother-in-law had been killed and my sister really needed me. I stayed with Robbie and little Will until my divorce was final, then…then I came here."

She sent him a smile, but he was still puzzling over the time line. She seemed to have left out a lot of parts. In particular, he found it odd that she would leave her Pennsylvania hometown for a secluded island off the South Carolina coast. He told her as much.

Brigit nodded, but she didn't answer right

away. Instead, stooped down to collect another shell, wiping away sand from its edges as she straightened. This one was dark gray with deep ridges fanning out from its base. Nothing about the shell would have prompted Kellen to give it a second look, much less pick it up, but apparently Brigit deemed it a keeper because she tucked it into the pocket of her shorts. They walked a little farther and she stopped for another shell, going through the same process before depositing it, too, in her pocket.

All the while, he waited, giving her time to fill in the blanks as she saw fit.

Finally, she did.

"I couldn't stay in my hometown."

"Too many bad memories," he guessed.

"Bad ones, yes, but good ones too, since that was where I grew up. But that wasn't why I left. Even after the divorce papers were signed and our marriage was officially over, Scott was still trying to control me.

"He started by begging me to come back. He told me I had misunderstood him. That if he was guilty of anything it was loving me too much. He wanted another chance to prove he had changed. I just wanted to move on. But everywhere I went, he would turn up. If I dropped off a dress at the dry cleaners, I'd walk out and find him in the parking lot. If I had a dentist appointment, he would be sitting in the waiting room. He started showing up at my mother's house unannounced, bringing her flowers and acting concerned for my well-being. She knew enough by that point that she could see through his act, but the rest of the town?" Brigit shook her head and sighed. "He'd used every angle he could think of to manipulate me and when none of them worked, he switched to manipulating public opinion."

"What do you mean?"

"Rumors started swirling around town that I had had an affair and that was why I'd left him and sought to end our marriage. He painted me as coldhearted and conniving. He even made me out to be anti-American."

"Anti-American?"

"Because he was a veteran. Trust me, the guy worked every angle he could think. He's still working them."

"Sounds as if you could write a book," Kellen said, trying to keep his reaction light even as he wanted to wrap his hands around the other man's throat and give it a good squeeze.

"Yeah. *I Was Married to a Sociopathic Stalker* Not sure whether it would be shelved in the non-fiction section of the library or with the horror titles. It was a nightmare."

"But you survived. And from what I can tell you're stronger than ever."

She tilted up her chin. "I am."

"That must tick him off but good."

"I'm sure it does." She smiled. Not at Kellen but at some unseen point in the distance. She was proud of herself, as well she should be.

Something occurred to Kellen then. Icy fingers danced up his spine as he asked, "Does your ex know where to find you?"

"I'm not in hiding," she replied somewhat in-dignantly. "I had to leave my hometown, but I'll be damned if he'll turn me into some kind of recluse. Besides, he never resorted to physica abuse."

Kellen nodded, all the while thinking that i

was only a short hop from controlling someone with words to controlling them using force.

"Have you considered a restraining order?" he asked.

"Considered it and did it." She sent him a droll look. "I'm not an idiot. My mother and sister took out restraining orders against him as well."

"Good."

"They still run into him from time to time, but at least he's stopped showing up at their homes. And I gave his photograph to all the ferry operators. They let me know whenever he's on his way over."

Despite the heat, those icy fingers were back. "Wait. Did you say *when*? He's been here?"

"He doesn't come as often as he used to, but yes. When I first took the job, he would show up once or twice a month. Now it's maybe once a season."

"So much for that damned restraining order," Kellen murmured.

"Oh, Scott honors it. He can't come within five hundred feet of the inn. One inch beyond that? He spreads out a blanket on the beach and settles in for the day, binoculars trained on the resort."

She shrugged, although Kellen saw through the casual gesture to the nerves below.

"I don't like it," he muttered.

"Neither do I, but since he's honoring the letter of the law, there's not much I can do about it."

Kellen disagreed. Sometimes a bully just needed to be bullied by someone else to finally get the picture. He might not be in any condition to pose a physical threat, but Lou cut an imposing figure. Maybe Kellen would ask his driver-slash-bodyguard to have a "chat" with Brigit's ex the next time the guy ventured onto Hadley Island.

Beside him, Brigit expelled a deep breath. "Anyway, that's my story. Are you sorry you asked?"

"No." And he wasn't. He used to avoid backstory where the women in his life were concerned, but he couldn't seem to learn enough about Brigit. "If I'm sorry about anything, it's that you had to go through all that."

They both had suffered devastating injuries, Kellen realized, albeit in different ways. Hers had been inflicted on her psyche. Since his were physical, they were more obvious, but that didn't make them more debilitating.

"Ready to turn back?" she asked.

Kellen was tired, but Brigit's sheer nerve had inspired him. Faced with adversity, she could have given up. She could have gone into hiding, living her life in seclusion to avoid being stalked. But she had done neither.

"Not quite yet," he told her. "Let's walk a little farther."

More than ever, he felt as if he had something to prove. To both of them.

CHAPTER TWELVE

BRIGIT SAT AT the desk in her cozy office. She'c set aside paperwork for something more sooth ing: a craft project involving the shells she'd beer collecting. She added the first layer to the bot tom of a cylindrical vase she'd picked up at a fle market after having no success in the storeroom All of the shells were in varying shades of gra and, as such, not particularly pretty. Which wa why she planned to alternate with layers of pal blue glass pebbles. When she finished half a hour later, she studied the final product in sat isfaction. Alone, the cheap vase, seashells an colored glass hadn't been much to look at, bu put together as they were, they had been trans formed into something attractive and interesting

Thinking of transformations, Kellen certainl had undergone one since his arrival on Hadle Island more than two months earlier. It was wel into August now, the heat outside almost intolerable even with the ocean's breeze. But he hadn't used that as an excuse to ease up on his rehabilitation efforts. Each evening he walked on the beach with Brigit. This despite his grueling daily workouts with Joe.

For the past several weeks, he'd pushed himself to the absolute limit, following his physical therapist's advice to the letter. His range of motion had improved vastly. His leg was stronger, more stable. Muscle tone had returned. Best of all, he claimed his pain level had moved to the tolerable range. He still needed a cane to get around, but he didn't complain.

Indeed, even more than his physical transformation was his emotional one. He seemed at peace with his situation even as he was still working hard to improve it. He appeared to have discovered a sense of purpose. It seemed like a lifetime ago that he'd last closeted himself in his room. In fact, he rarely stayed in the apartment for more than his workouts. Otherwise, he could be found out and about in the resort, greeting guests, fraternizing with his employees.

He'd won over Sherry easily enough with regular compliments for her evening dinner specials.

And he'd won over Brigit, even though she'd meant what she'd told him about not being in the market for a relationship.

In the market or not, how could she keep from falling for a man who appreciated her strength? Who viewed it as attractive? Who saw it not as a flaw to be exorcised, but a trait to be emulated?

But what the future held for the two of them was unclear. Kellen was healing, getting stronger by the day. That was the outcome she'd often wished for when he'd first arrived, because she'd been eager to see him leave. Now? Of course she was happy he'd improved so much in so short a period of time. But part of her couldn't help wondering what would happen when he felt he had recuperated enough. He loved the island, seemed to feel as connected to the resort as she did. But would he stay? And if he did, what would their relationship be then?

She fussed with the top layer of shells.

"That's pretty. You have a good eye."

She glanced up to find Kellen standing in the doorway. She hadn't heard his approach, another example of how much he had improved. His limp remained pronounced, but he no longer staggered and dragged his foot.

"Thanks."

"Where will you put this one?"

She made a humming sound. "I haven't decided yet. One of the guest rooms, most likely."

"Maybe I should start paying you a decorating fee."

A lopsided grin accompanied his words. His face was tanned from time spent outdoors and the corners of his mouth no longer turned down with pain. He was ridiculously handsome, even with his long hair. He hadn't had it cut since his arrival and the ends reached his collar. It gave him a dangerous vibe.

"I'll settle for dinner. Are you buying tonight?" She intended it as a joke. They often ate together in the inn's dining room.

"Actually, I am. I'd like to take you into Charleston for a meal."

"Charleston?"

"Unless you'd prefer someplace else."

"You want to take me out to dinner in Charleston," she repeated slowly.

"I do. But you can say no." He sobered. "Thi isn't business-related, Brigit. I'm asking you ou On a date."

A date.

Her heart took a flying leap off the high boar before diving straight to her toes. This was scary step. although not completely out of th blue. Something had been brewing between ther since that first kiss. But it had been easier to marginalize those feelings within the context of thei professional relationship. They were spending lot of time together. In fact, they were living together, albeit innocently enough.

Now he was making it clear he wanted something else…something more? As a professiona she urged herself to decline. Dating the boss wa never a good idea.

But she also was a woman. A woman wh found Kellen attractive and interesting and enjoyed spending time with him.

"I'd love to."

* * *

Brigit had almost forgotten what it was like to get dressed up for a night out. It had been more han a year since she'd last clocked out at the re-ort for a Saturday night. Her sister and nephew ad been visiting then, and, since it had been the ourth of July, the three of them had driven over o the opposite side of the island to watch the ireworks sprout up over Charleston. She dabbed little perfume in her cleavage, wondering what ind of fireworks she might be in for this night.

She'd gone with a dress and actual heels. Both vere several years old. She could only hope they vere still in style. It was that or her no-nonsense avy business suit and rounded-toe pumps. Her ister called as Brigit studied her reflection in the nirrored closet door of the guest room.

"I can't talk now," she told Robbie almost im-nediately, because once her sister got going it vas hard to get a word in edgewise.

"It's a Saturday night, Brig. You really need to nock off and kick up your heels once in a while. 'ut your boss on. I'll make him see reason."

Brigit had been purposely stingy with the de-

tails of her and Kellen's relationship. In part be
cause she hadn't been sure where it was heading
But also because she was afraid what her famil
would think. Scott had enjoyed a solid reputatio
in their community, and he'd still turned out t
be a total jerk behind closed doors. Meanwhile
Kellen's picture was probably in the dictionar
beside the word *womanizer.*

Still, she valued her sister's opinion. neede
her advice. And so Brigit let out the truth in
rush of words: "I'm going on a date with Ke
len tonight."

"What? Slow down and say that again."

Brigit took a deep breath and exhaled. "Kelle
and I are heading over to Charleston for dinne
in a little while. I'm getting ready right now."

"And it's a date?"

"Uh-huh." She glanced at her reflection, too
in the sleeveless pale blue sheath and strapp
sandals. "I'm wearing the dress I bought f
Will's christening. I don't have anything else i
my closet that's fancy enough. Do you think
still works?"

"It's a timeless piece. And the color is perfect
r you. It brings out your eyes."

"Thanks."

Brigit examined the eyes under discussion.
he'd added more liner than she usually went
ith. Same went for the mascara. Her eyes were
er best feature.

"Are you…nervous?" her sister asked.

"A little. I mean, it's a date, and I haven't had
ne of those in a long time." Actually, it wasn't
e date that had her nervous as much as what
ight come afterward. It had been even longer
nce she'd had sex. And lately, it was all she
ought about.

"It will be fine. Relax and enjoy yourself. I
uess I'm just a little surprised."

"Kellen and I have been spending a lot of time
gether, so it's not as if this came out of the
ue."

"Yet you've barely breathed a word of it to me,
en when I've asked you about him," Robbie
ot back. Her tone told Brigit she wasn't angry,
ut maybe a little hurt.

"I know. And I'm sorry. I just wanted to keep

this to myself for a while longer. I'm not su
what my feelings are, or his, so I wasn't reac
to examine them."

"And you're ready now?"

She fussed with her hair, which she had le
down for the occasion. No, she definitely wa
not. Here goes nothing, she thought.

"Well, I'm not looking for a fairy tale." She
gone that route once already and had lived to r
gret it. Her eyes were wide open this time. "I'
looking for a little…fun."

"That doesn't sound like you."

Brigit pictured her older sister frowning ar
had little doubt Robbie would be on the phor
with their mother as soon as they hung up.

Secretly, Brigit had to agree. A casual relatio
ship wasn't her style. But keeping things lig
and noncommittal seemed for the best. At lea
until she was certain of Kellen's intentions.

So she told Robbie, "Whatever happens b
tween Kellen and me, I'm not going to roma
ticize it."

"What do you mean by that?"

"Well, I know it won't lead to wedding bells

His track record with women told her so. As much as he'd changed in the past several weeks, surely he wasn't willing to give up his flashy lifestyle to hang around Faust Haven forever, even if the resort had been bequeathed to him by the grandfather he'd adored. "I'm not even sure that's where I would want it to lead anyway."

"Aw, honey. Don't let your experience with Scott sour you on marriage."

Brigit shot back, "You're one to talk. It's not as if you're out dating, and it's been how many years now since Mitch died?" She regretted the words as soon as they left her mouth. "I'm sorry, Robbie. That came out wrong. You know I just want you to be happy. As happy as you were with Mitch."

"I know. And I appreciate that. But our situations aren't the same. And not just because I'm a widow. I have Will to think about. Fair or not, I'm a package deal. A lot of the guys who might be interested in me aren't interested in a ready-made family."

"Then they're stupid."

"Totally," Robbie agreed without hesitation.

"And as such they aren't good enough to b
Will's stepdaddy. Now, back to you. You sa
you're not sure you're interested in a serious re
lationship. Okay, Brigit. I guess I can understar
that after all you've gone through. But what is
you *do* want?"

Needs. Wants. She'd been thinking about bo
a lot lately. And she still hadn't reached any fir
conclusions. She wanted to be happy. She wante
to be needed. Right now she was both. Cou
that be enough?

From the hallway, she heard the *tap-tap* of Ke
len's cane. He was coming to collect her for the
date. Excitement, not all of it sexual, bubbled
the surface, breaking her outward calm.

"What I'd love is a new dress," she told Rol
bie, even though she knew that wasn't what h
sister wanted to hear.

"Oh, come on!" Robbie complained. She wa
gearing up for what surely would have been a
inquisition when Brigit cut her off.

"I'm sorry, but I've got to go. We'll talk abo
this another time."

"Do you promise?"

"Yes."

Then Brigit opened the door and, despite all er talk about not romanticizing her relationship vith Kellen, one look at his handsome face and legant form and she knew she was lost.

Brigit stood framed in the doorway, a vision in ale blue silk that hugged her delicate curves. Although his gaze hadn't yet made it to her feet he new she was wearing heels, because her mouth vas now level with his chin. Kellen's heart exeuted the same dizzying flip it used to perform vhenever he'd stood at the top of a ski slope gazng down the run he was preparing to tackle.

This was better. And, at the same time, a hell f a lot scarier. Things were changing between nem. He was changing. And it wasn't just his ecovery.

"You look amazing," he told her. What other vomen spent hours trying to perfect, she'd chieved in barely one. He knew this because ne shower in the hall bathroom had been running when he'd passed it to go take his own.

"Thanks." She smiled and fussed with the ends

of her hair, looking uncertain, a description h
never thought he would ascribe to her. "You loc
pretty amazing, too."

He glanced at the dress pants, tie and buttor
down oxford. "I forgot what it was like to put c
something other than a T-shirts and track pant
I'm lucky I remembered how to tie a tie."

The Windsor knot at his throat suddenly fe
too tight, and that was before she laughed ar
tugged playfully at the strip of silk.

"I remember wondering where you'd wear a
the clothes that Lou hung in my closet that fir
day."

"I'm not sure why I packed them. Habit,
guess. But I'm glad I did now so I have som
thing suitable to wear for our dinner."

"I wouldn't care if you were in track pants ar
we were going to split a pizza on the beach," sh
told him.

Yes, Brigit would be fine with that. He ha
no doubt. But more than with any other woma
he'd known, Kellen wanted to impress her. H
wanted to show her a good time. Dazzle her a li
tle, even. If that made him shallow, so be it. B

ie thought a woman who'd been through what he had deserved a night to remember.

"I've got something better in mind than pizza. Do you like steak?"

She glanced over Kellen's shoulder. "Is Joe within earshot?"

He chuckled, realizing as he did so that he'd laughed more in the past few weeks than he had in the several months preceding them.

"No. He mentioned something about going to the kitchen to talk to Sherry about ways to lower the fat and sodium count in her recipes without sacrificing flavor. He took a notebook."

"Brave man," she murmured.

"Brave or stupid. But he should be okay. I think Sherry has a soft spot for him."

Brigit nodded. "It's impossible not to like Joe. He's a giant teddy bear."

"I'll tell you a secret. When I first got here and the two of you were all chatty and giggly—"

"Chatty and giggly? I think I'm offended," she asserted. But the flash of her smile contradicted her words.

"As I was saying, the two of you hit it off s
quickly that I felt a little left out."

"I seem to remember you accusing me of flir
ing with Joe."

"I did." Kellen nodded. "I was…jealous."

"You were not!" Her laughter rang out. Sh
thought he was joking.

"I didn't fully realize it at the time, but I wa
Jealous of the easy banter. Jealous of the insta
friendship. Wondering if maybe…" He ran h
fingers down one of her arms. Her expressio
sobered and she shivered.

Kellen stepped forward, bringing him full
into the spare room. Behind her, the futon wa
folded up, but he could picture Brigit on it, all
that glorious black hair spread over her pillov
case like spilled ink.

Only one wall separated the two of them
night. For weeks now he'd lain awake, his mi
taunting him with fantasies of the pair of the
together…at last. Other than stolen kisses a
hand-holding during walks, their relationsh
had remained as chaste as could be. He marvel
at his restraint, knowing that not all of it cou

e blamed on his bum leg. He was proceeding vith caution. Brigit wasn't one of his dalliances. Everything about her was different…special.

"I want you," he said softly. "More than I can ver remember wanting anyone."

He watched her eyes widen at his bold statement. He should have known it wouldn't throw er. Hell, he should have expected that she vouldn't be outdone.

"I feel the same way."

Kellen waited, expecting a "but" to enter the onversation, given their talk on the beach when he'd made it clear she wasn't ready to plow head with any sort of relationship. Instead, she ettled a hand on one slim hip and notched up her hin. One edge of the scar was visible. Overall, he cut had healed nicely, but it had yet to fade rom red to white. She didn't try to camouflage . Hell, she didn't seem bothered by it at all. Just s she accepted Kellen despite his scars and disbility. Or maybe even because of them.

She really was a most extraordinary woman.

He had plans for their evening. They included sumptuous meal at one of the area's newest

and most popular steakhouses. And a cham
pagne toast to the beginning of what he hope
would be a long relationship, because despite a
he'd learned about Brigit over the past coupl
months, he knew he'd only scratched the surfac
He wanted to know more. To know everythin
And even then he doubted he would ever gro
bored. At thirty-six, he'd finally grown up.

Hell, he might even be up for some dancin
during their evening out, as long as it was slo
and didn't involve too much movement. Finall
he'd planned to cap it off with a late-night stro
on the beach, so that they could be alone. H
intended to take a blanket, spread it out on th
sand, sit with her and count the stars. Then
maybe…

"We have…reservations," he managed.

"Do we? I have no reservations."

"No?"

He watched her swallow. With nerves? Or wit
need?

"None whatsoever."

His plans were forgotten the instant their lip
met. Even then, Kellen might have been abl

o summon up some willpower if she hadn't
vrapped his tie around her hand and drawn him
arther into the room. With their mouths still
used, she kicked the door closed behind him.
'he *snick* of the lock opened the floodgates. A
idal wave of pent-up need flowed out.

No words were necessary as she walked back-
vard toward the futon, pulling Kellen along by
iis tie. He didn't mind being led. Vaguely, he was
.ware of his cane falling to the floor, the clatter
f wood meeting wood all but lost to the blood
oaring in his ears. His hands were locked on her
vaist, not merely for support, but to let her take
he lead. She needed to be in control. He got that.
\nd he was happy to accommodate her.

Brigit let go of the end of his tie, but only so
he could free it from its knot. She yanked the
ength of silk from around his neck with a flour-
sh, triumph gleaming in her blue eyes as she sent
t sailing through the air. Then she tugged the
hirt from his pants and started in on the placket
f buttons with what he considered maddening
lowness. Left to him, Kellen simply would have

rent the fabric and sent the buttons flying. Sh
was much more practical…and patient.

What seemed like an eternity later, she finall
finished. The heat of her hands singed his ski
as she spread open the shirt and pushed it o
his shoulders. He had to lower his arms so tha
it could drop to the floor, joining his discarde
cane and tie on the hardwood. Her fingertip
trailed over the bare skin of his chest and sh
kissed the shoulder that had been dislocated i
his accident. It hadn't bothered Kellen in month
but he groaned now, suffering an exquisite form
of pain as her mouth trailed along his collarbon
and then cruised south to his nipple. She passe
her tongue around it before meeting his gaze.

"How are you holding up?" she asked softly.

"Ready to combust," he admitted.

She smiled slyly. "I meant your leg. You'v
been standing unsupported for a few minute
now."

"I wouldn't mind lying down." His smile wa
every bit as cunning.

"Let's get you out of those pants first."

The breath backed up in his throat, but h

inally managed to exhale. He fingered the soft ilk of her dress. “What about you?”

“We’ll get to me in a moment. Right now, I’m ndressing you. Is that a problem?”

“Not at all.”

“Good.” And she reached for his belt.

Never had Brigit been this forward, acted this oldly. Of course, she had little practice with eduction. Other than Scott, she’d only been in-imate with one other man. A boy really, since he act had occurred after her high school prom. All of her experiences with sex had been, well, lisappointing.

She was positive that was about to end. Kellen vasn’t a boy. He was all man. And eager, if the rection straining against his fly was any indi-ation. But unlike her ex, he wasn’t telling her vhat he wanted from her or how she was sup-osed to act or criticizing her for doing some-hing wrong. Kellen was allowing her to be in he driver’s seat, and she planned to enjoy every econd of the ride.

She slipped the pants down his legs and sat

on the edge of the futon so that she could hel
him step out of them. Another time, she woul
have taken a moment to fold them to prevent th
fabric from wrinkling. But just as she had wit
his shirt and tie, she left them where they were
Other matters were taking precedence. Namel
getting out of her dress.

Kellen's hands found the zipper in the back
He lowered it to between her shoulder blade
but couldn't continue without leaning over, a fea
complicated by his bad leg. She corrected th
matter by standing.

A moment later, they were both naked, thei
breaths coming in heavy gasps as, bodies presse
tight, they strained to get closer still.

"I think we'd better get you off your feet," sh
told him. The words came out between pantin
breaths.

"I think so, too."

Together they lowered onto the futon.

CHAPTER THIRTEEN

'OE WAS SITTING in the living room when they
:merged from Brigit's bedroom forty minutes
ater. Lou was next to him on the couch. Both
nen were drinking iced tea while they watched
a baseball game. Other than offering a greeting
vhen she and Kellen entered the living room,
ıeither of the men said a word.

Brigit, however, took one look at Kellen's wrin-
:led clothes and satisfied expression and knew
t had to be obvious what the pair of them had
)een up to.

She wanted to be embarrassed. It wasn't like
ıer to behave so…so what? The possible an-
;wers seemed endless. She narrowed it down
o three—spontaneously, wantonly and reck-
essly—and couldn't stop a smile from turning
ıp the corners of her lips.

"Keep grinning like that, sweetheart, and

everyone will know what we've been up to," Kellen whispered in her ear.

"Yes, and they'll be envious. *Really, really* envious," she whispered back. To which he chuckled.

Lou pushed to his feet. "Ready to go now,
boss?"

"Yes."

The driver nodded. "I'll bring the Escalad
around and meet you at the main door."

Joe rose as well and pulled a slip of paper from
his pants pocket. "I took the liberty of callin
the restaurant, Mr. F, and jotted down a few c
the menu's healthiest selections." He handed th
note to Kellen while adding, "I'd stick with fish
The grilled salmon in particular sounds excellent. And it has all of those healthy omega-threes
Just don't let them douse it in any kind of sauce.

"Salmon?" Kellen's mouth puckered on th
word as if he were sucking on a sourball. "It's
steakhouse, Joe."

"You know how I feel about red meat."

"I do."

"And haven't you gotten healthier and stronger following my regimen?"

"I have."

Joe nodded, as if the matter was resolved. "None of the selections I wrote down contain monosodium glutamate, but I'd ask the server to hold it anyway, just to be on the safe side."

"Hold the MSG. Got it," Kellen replied in a dutiful tone that didn't fool Brigit one bit. This was merely the path of least resistance.

"And remember, baked potato instead of fries, and watch the dressing for your salad. Lots of hidden fat there, not to mention sodium. I suggest requesting vinegar and olive oil, and go light on the oil."

Kellen still had about a dozen pounds to gain back to put him at his optimum weight, but Joe remained adamant that he wanted him to do it the healthy way.

"Fish, no sauce. Salad, no dressing. Potatoes baked not fried. Can't wait to dig in," he muttered.

Kellen tucked the paper in his pants pocket,

where Brigit was fairly certain it would stay fo
the remainder of the evening.

Sebastian's Steakhouse was located in a ren
ovated three-story building on Broad Street i
Charleston's historic downtown. They were lat
for their reservation, but a fifty-dollar bill slippe
to the maître d' apparently smoothed over an
problem.

The first two stories of the restaurant wer
open to all diners. The third, which was wher
they were seated, was reserved for A-list guest
only. Brigit had never eaten at Sebastian's, re
gardless of the floor. And it was no wonder, sh
decided as she studied the à la carte menu. Th
prices were well beyond her budget.

No sooner had they sat down at their table tha
a black-vested server arrived with a tray carry
ing two champagne flutes and bottle of Dom i
a silver ice bucket.

"Shall I pour?" he asked Kellen.

"Please."

This was Kellen's lifestyle, she realized. A
dazzled by it as she felt, it also represented

world she knew little about. A world to which he would be returning at some point in the not-so-distant future. The thought threatened to tarnish the luster of the evening, so she shoved it away.

"Enjoy," the waiter said before leaving.

Once they were alone again, Kellen said, "I had plans to sweep you off your feet tonight. An amazing meal, maybe even a little dancing."

"Really?" The latter came as a surprise. A welcome one, since it showed how far he'd come.

"Really. Instead, I'm the one who's been swept off my feet." He raised his glass. "By you."

She clinked the rim of her champagne flute against his. "I'd say it was mutual."

They caught one of the last ferries back to Hadley Island. Lou had the radio on a jazz station. Brigit sat snuggled up to Kellen's side in the backseat. The Escalade's high beams illuminated the surroundings as they returned to the resort. Their night out was ending.

Joe was asleep on the sofa bed in the living room, snoring softly as they made their way past

him to the hallway. At her bedroom door, Bri
git stopped.

"I guess this is where we say good-night." Sh
smiled.

Kellen's expression remained serious. "Doe
it have to be?"

It was exactly what she'd been hoping to hea
although her previous boldness had ebbed, pre
venting her from saying as much.

She took the hand he offered. Together the
walked to the bedroom at the end of the hall. A
they stepped over the threshold she knew tha
much more than their sleeping arrangements fo
the night had changed.

CHAPTER FOURTEEN

)NLY A WEEK of the official summer season emained. Once Labor Day passed, children vould head back to school and parents would tart hoarding their vacation days to use on their :ids' breaks.

The island would be quieter without all of the amilies, life a little slower until the snowbirds tarted arriving in November, eager to leave the :old weather of the north behind for a couple veeks or even months.

Brigit would be happy for the break. She was ɔoking forward to taking a little time off. In paricular, she wanted to spend it with Kellen doing vhatever they wanted to do.

The past couple weeks had been a lovely blur f stolen moments during the day and unbriled passion at night. The depth of her feelings mazed her. Falling for her boss hadn't been her

intention, but that was what had happened. She'
tumbled headlong into love.

It terrified her, but she couldn't deny she wa
happy. Happier than she'd been in years. Eve
though he hadn't said so, she was certain Ke
len felt the same. His every glance, touch an
expression told her so. When they made love,
was perfect. A union of souls as much as bodie
She smiled as she laid on the bed that had bee
hers, then his and now was theirs. The two
them had been sharing it since the night of the
dinner in Charleston.

It was only six o'clock, but Kellen was alread
awake and up. He'd told her to wait for him i
bed and he would be back in a few minutes wit
a surprise.

Just as she'd learned to be spontaneous an
go with the flow, Brigit had learned to apprec
ate surprises. Especially Kellen's. The other da
he had surprised her with a bouquet of roses,
good two dozen of the long-stemmed red var
ety. They were in a vase on the nightstand, the
fragrance perfuming the air even as their velvet
petals had begun to wilt.

And just the day before, he'd had his mother
nd stepfather out to the island to dinner. Bri-
it had assumed the invitation was to begin re-
toring their relationship and she'd been proud
f him for extending an olive branch. Pride had
hanged to shock when he'd insisted that Brigit
ine with them. And shock had morphed into
n emotion too huge to name when he'd intro-
uced her as his girlfriend rather than as the inn's
nanager. She smiled at the memory and, grow-
ng impatient for his return, called out, "What's
aking you so long?"

"Perfection takes time," came his reply from
own the hall.

"I don't need perfection. What I need, all I
vant, is you!"

She threw her arms wide as she made the dec-
aration, only to have her hand connect with the
oses. The flowers, vase and all, tumbled to the
loor, water soaking a portion of the area rug be-
ore sloshing over the hardwood. "Shoot!"

She opened the drawer in the nightstand, where
he kept a box of tissues. Grabbing a handful,
he sopped up what she could. Afterward, she

straightened, intending to throw the sodden mes
in the garbage. The manila envelope caught he
eye. Her name was printed on the outside. Wher
had it come from? She certainly hadn't put i
there. Which could only mean that Kellen hac
But why? What was it? She reached for it an
opened the flap. The soggy tissues were forgot
ten as she looked over the document she'd pulle
from inside.

She swallowed in disbelief as the words regis
tered and her heart broke. No! No! This couldn
be right. But it was all there in black and white
Kellen's plan to dismiss her.

It was mere minutes later, although it felt lik
a lifetime, when Kellen filled the doorframe an
called, "Surprise! Breakfast in bed."

He held a tray laden with two plates of Belgia
waffles, sliced fresh strawberries and a pair c
coffee cups. A small bouquet of daisies spille
from a squat square vase. As distraught as sh
was, it barely registered that he was standin
unsupported, cane nowhere to be found. At th
moment, the only thing Brigit was aware of wa
the terrible ache in her chest.

Surprise, indeed.

He'd planned to let her go. All this time she'd een trying not to worry about whether he would eave again or where their burgeoning relation-hip was heading. It had never occurred to her e might stay and she would be the one packing er bags.

Give him the benefit of the doubt, her head ar-ued. But the busted up heart that had only re-ently healed, had her holding up the document nd asking coolly, "When were you going to pring this surprise on me?"

He blinked in confusion for a moment. Was nat proof that he didn't know what she was talk-ng about? Or proof that he was just like Scott? first-class liar and manipulator. His face paled nd a guilty grimace replaced his easy smile. She ook that as her answer, and wondered how else e had deceived her.

"Where did you get that?" he asked.

"It was in the nightstand. You'll forgive me or opening it. After all, the envelope was ad-ressed to me."

"Brigit, it's not what it looks like." He limped

into the room. Coffee sloshed over the rim of th
cups on the tray as he set it down on the be
where just that morning they'd made love.

How original, she thought. And how utter
untrue. "It looks like a severance package. A
you going to tell me I'm wrong about that?"

"No. You're not wrong. That's what it is. Whe
I first came back, my thought was eventual
to take over running the resort myself. I didn
think you'd want to stay on given that your du
ties would be reduced, but I'd planned to ask."

"How nice of you to give me the option," sh
drawled.

"I sounds bad, I know, but things changed. Yo
have to believe me, I had it drawn up month
ago. Long before you and I—"

"Had sex," she stated flatly, even though th
words left her feeling sick.

"Don't say it like that. Please."

"How should I say it, Kellen?" she demande
"That's what it was, right? Sex. With my boss
"It was more than that. It *is* more than that
he insisted.

"You lied to me. Are you going to deny that?

"If I lied to anyone, Brigit, it was myself. When ur relationship began to change, I didn't trust ıy feelings for you."

But she wouldn't hear it. She couldn't believe . "It all comes down to this, Kellen. Once you ad your fun, you planned to let me go." Her yes blurred again as she studied the document. You're very generous, by the way. I've been vell compensated for my…service."

Her stomach threatened to heave on the last vord. All of the beauty she'd found in their love-ıaking became sordid. Used, that was how she elt now. And stupid, because all of her internal ectures about keeping things casual and enjoy-ıg the moment had been a load of baloney. She'd allen in the love with Kellen. She should have nown better.

She ran from the room, not stopping when he alled her name. She couldn't stay. Couldn't bear o hear more lies. She was at the apartment door, ngers curled around the handle when she heard crash followed by an oath. That alone wouldn't ave stopped her. But the ensuing sob that pre-ented Brigit from opening the door.

She tiptoed back through the living room an
peeked down the hallway. Kellen was sprawle
face down on the floor just outside the spar
room. He wasn't trying to get up. His face wa
pressed into his crossed arms, shoulders shak
ing. He was crying.

"Kellen?"

He raised his head. His face was damp, eye
red. "I thought you were gone."

"I was worried you'd hurt yourself," she lie
"Are you okay?"

He pushed up until he was able to bring h
legs around into a sitting position with his bac
against the wall. "No. I'm not okay, Brigit."

"I'll get Joe."

Before she could turn, however, Kellen hel
out his hand. "I need you."

She swallowed. He'd told her that before. "B
you're letting me go."

Arm still outstretched, he replied, "Never!
know it looks that way from the document, b
I had it made up months ago, the day of m
disastrous appointment with the specialist i
Charleston."

She recalled the interest he'd shown in the daily perations. His interactions with the staff. "You anted to run it with me out of the picture."

"If you wouldn't stay." He nodded. "Yes. When ny grandfather left me this place that was his ish. But Brigit—"

She continued to ignore his outstretched hand, nd instead demanded, "When were you going tell me about your plans?"

Kellen closed his eyes and let his hand drop his side. "I didn't have a firm date in mind. hen, I just… forgot about it."

"We're talking about my future. How could ou *forget* something as big as this?" she de-nanded, shaking the sheaf of papers in front of er.

"You," Kellen stated simply. Half of his mouth ose and some of her pain lifted with it. "You nade me forget a lot of things, Brigit. Like how be bitter and angry and hopeless. And you ught me a lot, too."

"Like how to manage a resort?" she asked, hough the question carried no heat.

"Like how to believe in myself. Like how

not only to accept my life as it was, but how t
dream new dreams. And I have. I'm dreaming
a different future. Here at the resort." He pause
"With you. I love you."

Love. The word threatened to snatch her brea
away. "You didn't say anything," she said slowl
cautiously.

"That's because I've never been in love b
fore. I've used the word with other women, b
I never felt like this. I wanted to be sure, and
am. But—"

"But what?"

"Well, you had been in love before. So muc
so you got married. Your ex-husband used th
word, but mangled its meaning. He hurt you
badly, made you doubt yourself… I didn't thi
you'd trust the word alone, so I've been tryi
to show you how I felt instead."

Brigit swallowed. He was right, of course. S
wouldn't have trusted the mere word, as potent
she found it to be now. But actions spoke clear
and left no room for second-guessing.

And so Kellen had been showing her, reveali
his true feelings to her in gestures big and sma

How different this man was from the brooding nd broken self-involved heir who'd first darkned her door and had turned her life upside own with his edicts and demands.

"You love me." She whispered the words, ugged them close as she dropped down beside im on the floor.

"More each day," he replied, reaching for her. Tell me you'll stay. I want you with me always. want Faust Haven to be our home. This resort be ours to run together. I don't want a fuire that doesn't include you. Please, tell me you on't leave."

Brigit framed his face with her hands, kissed is damp cheeks. The last pieces of her broken eart fitted together and fused, leaving it whole. inally.

"I won't leave, Kellen. Ever. I love you, too." ist before their mouths met, she whispered. You are my future."

* * * * *

MILLS & BOON®

Large Print – May 2015

THE SECRET HIS MISTRESS CARRIED
Lynne Graham

NINE MONTHS TO REDEEM HIM
Jennie Lucas

FONSECA'S FURY
Abby Green

THE RUSSIAN'S ULTIMATUM
Michelle Smart

TO SIN WITH THE TYCOON
Cathy Williams

THE LAST HEIR OF MONTERRATO
Andie Brock

INHERITED BY HER ENEMY
Sara Craven

TAMING THE FRENCH TYCOON
Rebecca Winters

HIS VERY CONVENIENT BRIDE
Sophie Pembroke

THE HEIR'S UNEXPECTED RETURN
Jackie Braun

THE PRINCE SHE NEVER FORGOT
Scarlet Wilson